The Bride Least Wanted

Rebecca De Medeiros

Books by Rebecca De Medeiros

Brides of Liberty, Texas series

———————————

A Bargain Bride
A Betting Bride
The Bride Least Wanted

Hired Husbands Series

———————————

Shotgun Groom

Heroes at Heart Series

———————————

Toddlers and Tycoons
A Family Man

Dedicated to Terri Erickson, my friend and fellow warrior.

It has been an honor to drudge away three days a week alongside of you. You may never read these words, but you made the last two years of my life bearable, and for that, I thank you. When others have turned their backs, you were there. You amaze me with your strength and your kindness. I am humbled to call you my friend. The world needs more Terri Ericksons… don't be mad at me for the shout out. I know you are shy, but it's your turn to be praised. You are one beautiful soul that I have the upmost respect for.

I want to be just like you, when I finally do grow up.

Also, to all of those battling cancer, never let anyone tell you that your time is limited... keep fighting, even if it's just to prove the statistics wrong. Life is the most precious gift we've been given, never give up on it. Miracles happen every day, a cure will come.

Prologue

Texas, 1869

The beauty of the day mocked him.

There was nary a cloud in the sky to block the sun from shining down upon the crisp, fertile green fields that lay before him. A slight breeze blew in the air helping to keep the late August sun from becoming too unbearable. Sadly, Mathias Sinclair could not fully appreciate the relief.

As he stood with his back to his visitor, contemplating the bright blue sky, he wished it were storming instead. It would've better suited his mood had the heavens been brewing thunderclouds. A deluge at the very least should mark the day that a man's world came to an end.

Mathias pressed a torn and bloodied hand to the back of his neck, trying to rub some of his soreness away and chuckled sardonically.

He'd been working all morning on a small plot of land off to the right of the house, struggling to even the ground for a suitable garden. He'd intended it to be a surprise for his new bride, but found himself doing more damage to his hands than to the stubborn ground. When the wagon first pulled up, Mathias had been grateful for the interruption. Quick as a wink, he'd released his grip on the pull harness and foolishly hurried forward to greet the dark haired woman waiting. All too eager to receive his soon- to- be sister by marriage, that he'd nearly tripped over his big feet to get to her.

Mathias should have known by the look on her weary face that the news wouldn't have been to his liking. And yet still, he'd been blindly hoping that the woman had come bearing the news that his sweetheart Daisy had finally come to her senses and returned home to him.

Apparently, she hadn't, and he was a damn fool for holding out hope.

As all of his dreams crumbled at his feet, Mathias wondered why it didn't hurt more, why he wasn't angrier. Instead of fury, he felt this strange numbness settle inside the center of his chest.

"I'm sorry to be the one telling you this. I know it would be better hearing this coming from Papa—"

The soft voice that spoke from behind barely registered within him, as Mathias narrowed his eyes and concentrated on the slight movement of cattle in the distance.

Alec, his friend and partner, was learning to herd. Even from here, Mathias could tell things weren't going the way Alec wanted them to. Mathias could almost make out the curses flying out of his friend's mouth. Any other time, Mathias would've been laughing his hind end off, but at the moment mirth was the last thing that he was feeling.

"Mr. Sinclair?"

"I built this for her. All of it… for her." His voice hadn't so much as cracked as he said the words, but Mathias felt them burn like bile as they spilled past his lips. It was hard to admit the lengths he'd gone to please his promised bride.

With the tip of his boot he kicked away a stray pebble lying near his foot. He'd wanted to build his new wife a life that she'd always dreamt of. The last fifteen months had been back breaking, but Mathias had finally succeeded in building the extravagant house and main outbuilding that he'd planned to use to store the feed for the few head of cattle that he'd purchased.

Alec had tried to tell him that he was crazy for going to such extremes, but Mathias hadn't listened. Daisy had always wanted the finest house in the territory, how could he refuse her dream?

Hiring on Patrick Culver to help get the spread up and running, Mathias had been working day and night to ready the ranch. There weren't enough funds as of yet to hire more men, so the three men tried in vain to put in more hours than there were in a day. Annie, Patrick's wife, offered to work in his kitchen to help feed the men while they worked, but lately she had taken on more chores as well. Mathias would have to find a way to pay the woman, though he knew she would never outright demand it from him, as Annie was skittish around just about anyone who wasn't her husband.

With plans to slowly build the herd and add onto the ranch within the next year when the place finally began to see a bit of a profit, Mathias had set about adding touches that he'd thought a new bride would appreciate.

Why the hell couldn't she have waited to see him succeed before figuring him for a failure? He'd just needed a bit more time. He could have made her happy.

As Mathias looked out over the land that he'd chosen to claim as his own, he should have felt pride. Instead, he only felt empty inside.

The rustling of skirts swished as the caller moved closer and cleared her throat delicately. "Mr. Sinclair?" she murmured, obviously feeling the need to remind him of her presence. As if he could forget that he had a witness to his humiliation.

"Yes, Miss Etta?"

"I'm...I'm so sorry Mr. Sinclair," Etta Howard consoled him in a quiet voice.

He felt her small hand briefly land upon his arm, but as he turned to face her, she quickly snatched it back. The little woman was once again wringing her hands.

Etta's wary countenance hadn't changed since she'd first arrived to deliver the news to him. Mathias knew that she was waiting for the 'giant' to lose his temper, and from the looks of her, she would be ready to run when he did so.

As long as he'd known the Howards, Etta had always been timid. But even so, it still bothered him. Mathias hated that his massive size made people cautious around him. Even his beautiful Daisy had claimed his calloused hands too large, too rough, to touch her fragile skin.

"It's a grand home and the land is beautiful, but Daisy won't be coming home. She's…" Etta trailed off uncomfortably.

"*She's what*?" Mathias asked her harshly. Though, truth be told, he probably already knew the answer.

"Daisy's married." Etta rushed out.

No, he couldn't have guessed that…

Daisy was married? He'd never have expected that declaration to pour forth from Etta's mouth. Daisy wasn't happy; Daisy didn't love him…yes. Daisy married someone else…never. And just when the hell had she met the man? She'd only been gone four months!

Mathias watched as Etta hastily took two steps back. Her eyes grew round and a horrified expression crossed her face, as she gripped a handful of her dull, homespun skirts. The flash of the worn tipped boots she wore, reminded Mathias all too well of how different she was from her sister.

Etta was soft and unobtrusive, while Daisy was all glitter and excitement. His intended had always complained that she wanted to be more than just a dirt farmer's daughter. Her sister on the other hand, seemed to like if not gladly accept the life she'd been given. A bitter laugh welled in his chest as Mathias realized that he should have picked the younger Howard daughter to court instead. At least Etta would have gone through with the deed.

Flighty, bright eyed Daisy was too wild to be tamed. He should've known better.

"I'm so sorry...we just received the news ourselves. We will certainly repay the money that you loaned to Papa before he died," Etta hurriedly assured him. "It will just take us some time to gather the funds."

There was a cold ache in his chest and Mathias rubbed at it absently as he turned to face the woman standing at his side. He slowly exhaled a ragged breath and unclenched his fists.

"Thank you for informing me," he muttered with as much politeness as he could muster up.

"Mr. Sinclair, I—"

Mathias held one massive palm outward halting her. It wasn't Etta's fault that her sister had decided to flee instead of becoming his bride. Daisy Lynn always had a mind of her own, and Mathias actually felt bad for the plain young woman that had been left to clean up after her selfish sister. But he couldn't stand there and listen to Etta Howard's apologies any longer.

After mumbling an appropriate response to her, Mathias respectfully guided the tiny woman to her cart and helped her into the shabby wagon. The waiting nag attached to the rickety cart shifted uneasily as he reached out a hand to pat her dappled ashen coat. The poor girl had seen better days and was much too skinny, confirming his suspicions. The Howards were barely making do on their tiny farm; there was no way that Mathias could ask for the return of the money that he'd given Daisy's father. His ranch would just have to survive without the funds.

"Tell your Ma not to worry about the money," he ordered gruffly. "You both owe me no debt."

"For what it's worth, I think Daisy was a fool," Etta, head bowed, murmured before clicking her tongue and setting the cart in motion.

Mathias had put blood, sweat, and every last bit of his money into building Daisy the fancy home that she'd claimed to long for. But in the end, it was all pointless. Just like all of the promises they'd made to each other, it was empty, and she was gone.

In all the time that Mathias had been away riding with the Rangers, dreaming about the life he'd have with her when he came home, not once had he worried that Daisy wouldn't follow through with the wedding. He'd certainly not expected her to bolt the way she had.

He hadn't seen it coming, and for that Mathias felt like a buffoon. Why hadn't he realized the truth before now? What had he missed along the way? Daisy had seemed happy, hadn't she? She'd gone along with the plans that their mothers had been hatching while he'd been away.

Now like a dupe, Mathias was forced to stand by and watch as the Howard family wagon pulled away.

Never again, he silently promised himself as he walked back to the strip of land he'd been tilling and got back to work ripping up the ground. Never again would he play the fool for a woman. No woman was worth the risk of a broken heart. No woman was worth begging for…

That day Mathias Sinclair lost his faith in women. Walling up his heart, he swore that he'd never fall into that trap called love.

This is the story of how one woman with a bit of determination and one misaimed bullet restored that faith, and made him regret his promise. As with all good men, sometimes it just takes patience and a slap of desire upside the head for them to recognize just what they need.

-Foolish are those, which fight against fate-

CHAPTER ONE

December, 1873

Gertrude Bixby was in a foul temper.

As she strode heavily down the boardwalk on her trek through the small town, it was all she could do to not shake her fists at the sky and commit blasphemy. It wasn't fair this position she'd been put into, and although Trudy was far from happy about it, there was no other alternative.

The heels of her new half boots clicked loudly against the wooden planks as she made her way over to her father's bank. The heavy bustle of her walking dress bounced rapidly with each furious step that she took, and Trudy battled the urge to reach back and whack the errant puff into submission. To do so would only draw more curious stares, and she had enough eyes upon her as it was.

The chilly December air bit into her and she shivered. Trudy had been in such a rush that she hadn't taken the time to don her fur lined overcoat before setting out on her destination. Wishing that she'd worn a heavier frock, she fought against the urge to turn back. She couldn't give in to the temptation, for fear that she'd turn coward and give up on her quest.

"Lands' sakes!" she cried out as the slight train of her dress caught on one uneven plank, halting her mid stride.

As gently as she could, Trudy tried to pry the material free, but the ivory lace trim clung to the nail stubbornly. Trudy was forced to stop and yank the on the hem of the material before she could stomp on. "Blazes!" she huffed when the delicate material tore as it came free, further irritating her. She had liked this dress, the pale color was her favorite, and now it was ruined.

"You in a passel of trouble over thar' Miss Trudy?" a booming voice called out. The meddlesome Beans Paterson, no doubt. The old man seemed to be under the impression that she would choose to converse with him after he'd saddled her with the nickname, *Snooty Sal*. Trudy ignored him, as she surveyed the damage to her skirts. She would show him snooty.

Trudy knew she was fodder for gossips and always would be. For entertainment she lived up to their estimations of her as a way to snub her nose at them all. It had become a game to her, to see how far she could push her outlandish behavior.

Paying no attention to the curious stares of the onlookers, she muttered under her breath and continued walking on.

With one last grumble, she shrugged off the loss of the garment, figuring that she would just order a similar gown made later in the day. She was due a new wardrobe soon anyhow, as the women of Liberty had already started to copy this new dress style of hers. It was the heavy burden of a society leader, always having to set the standards of ladies attire. The pattern books took nearly a year to come from Paris, and Trudy was tired of waiting to be dressed as if she were a fluffy decoration. Unfortunately, her father demanded that she be, and the consequences would be harsh if she failed him. For Trudy's every action represented the man himself, or so he believed. Dressing poorly was a greater sin to him.

"Morning Miss Trudy!" the barber called out as she passed him on the street. Trudy also paid him little mind. She was on a mission to stop her father before things progressed any farther than they had already, and had no time for idle chatter.

As she clutched the slim, leather bound ledger that she'd stolen from her father's study in her grasp, she felt ill at the thought of its contents. Frankly, she was surprised that the damnable evidence hadn't burned right through the delicate lace of her glove and scorched the skin of her hand.

She sighed with relief as she finally approached her destination. In a few moments, she'd have the truth she sought.

With a mighty shove, the bank doors crashed open and Trudy burst in. She quickly ran past a group of women standing in line and came to a halt next to a filthy man standing at the counter. Pushing him aside, she pounded one gloved fist on the wide polished counter.

"Hey!" the grimy man snapped at Trudy's discourteous shoving.

No- good- Joe Vernon smelled about as rank as he looked, and Trudy figured that she'd have to burn the beautiful gloves she'd worn. This day was proving to be very destructive in regards to her clothing.

"Get my father," Trudy brusquely ordered the waiting teller, ignoring Joe's squawk of indignation. She had no time for niceties.

"Yes Miss Bixby. Right away," the bank clerk uttered even as Joe demanded that he stay where he was.

"Go, now," Trudy snapped when the thin man hesitated.

With a gulp, the poor clerk hastily complied with her command, nearly tripping over the wooden stool he'd been sitting on as he hurried to do her bidding. Obviously, he was more afraid of gaining her ire than angering the dirty Joe. This pleased Trudy greatly, so she darted Joe a smug smile and watched as his face become purple with rage. The man muttered something venomous in return, but Trudy chose to turn her back on him. She couldn't stomach Joe in the least, and couldn't care less as to what he had to say. He was nothing but a local bully, a man who sometimes did odd jobs for her father, and more oft than not, had one finger within his nose and his other hand scratched his man parts.

While Trudy waited for her father to attend her, she cast a glance about the room. The white washed walls of the building would soon need a new coating and the wooden counters a good polishing. Trudy wondered why her father hadn't noticed the flaws as of yet. It was unlike him to not have had someone's head for the neglect. Her papa was nothing if not a stickler for appearances.

The bank was busy today, she noted. Papa should be pleased with the turnout, which would only aid Trudy in her confrontation. A content Thomas Bixby meant that it was less likely that she'd be wearing bruises by the day's end.

Heading the line of ladies evidently awaiting their turn at the teller was Melody O'Malley. The woman was heavy with child and looked quite uncomfortable with her condition, as a child clung to her skirts. Trudy inclined her head to the matron and pretended that she didn't feel the slightest twinge of hurt as Mrs. O'Malley feigned unawareness of her presence.

Trudy couldn't really blame Melody, as she hadn't been too friendly toward the poor woman when she'd first come to town as a catalogue bride for Gabriel O'Malley. Of course, Trudy wasn't nice to very many people; her papa would never allow that. Papa had high standards for his family, and there'd be hell to pay if Trudy didn't stick to them. Thomas hand-picked his daughter's acquaintances and when the ragged woman and her young sister had come to town, he'd promptly snubbed his nose at the pair.

Standing behind Melody was mousy Etta Howard. The poor dear was wearing a dress that Trudy wouldn't dress a hog in. The gray material was so dowdy that it was barely fit for a washerwoman's rags. Trudy longed to gift the unfortunate spinster with one of her castoffs, but she feared her papa's reaction. Along with his snobbery, Thomas Bixby hadn't been born with a single charitable bone in his portly body.

The last woman in line moved slightly forward, placing herself in between Etta and Melody as if to protect them from Trudy's usual spitefulness. Trudy wrinkled her nose as her gaze landed on Serena Wentworth, her adversary.

Any other time, Trudy would have made a cutting remark to the flame haired woman to get her goat, but today, she just couldn't find the pluck to do so. Trudy was just plain tired of it all. Their rivalry had come to a head in any case. After the irritating woman had married the man that Trudy had set her sights on, there really was nothing left to compete for.

She was actually glad that the mayor had settled on Serena instead, for she truly hadn't wanted to marry him anyway. It had only been part of her papa's plan. A plan, that Trudy had been a fool to go along with. Alec Wentworth, while handsome as sin, failed to stir her blood.

Moreover, it was hard to continue to act as if you were better than another, when your father himself was a traitor… or so Trudy had just recently learned.

Of course, Trudy *had* recently spun turncoat herself, when she'd gone to Serena's brother, Mathias Sinclair, and informed him of what her father had done with his parents' money. So, who was she to throw stones?

Her father's treachery was just too much to swallow this time. How could he have done this to the town…to their family? How could she have unknowingly helped him do this? Even Trudy had more scruples than to allow herself to be a part of this dastardly scheme. She may have done some wicked things to please her papa in the past, but this was beyond the pale. This scheme was pure evil and needed to be stopped.

How had her father's greed gotten so out of hand, and what had he been doing with the money? Didn't he care how his actions would affect his family?

Trudy knew all too well that her father kept mistresses, but did he need to steal from local families to support his peccadilloes? The questions just kept popping into her mind until Trudy thought that she'd scream unless she got some answers. So she had set out and done just that. Throwing caution to the wind, she'd snooped into her father's private affairs. Only, the answers that she'd sought had brought about more questions to be answered. Nothing had added up.

As Trudy tapped her toe anxiously upon the wooden planked flooring waiting for her father to attend her, she contemplated the mess that she'd found herself in. While she was torn between what had been the right thing to do, she still felt as if she had destroyed her father in the process. Guilt was something new for her. Trudy had never before stopped to consider her own actions and she was not overly fond of the feeling.

It was only yesterday that Trudy had gone and lost all of her sensibilities. Arranging to meet a Sinclair, of all people, in a saloon, of all places! She must have been mad to think that the man would help her. The Bixby's and the Sinclair's hadn't been what most folks would call on 'friendly' terms. Mathias Sinclair had no reason to believe anything that came out of her mouth. If the tables were turned, Trudy doubted she would've trusted him either.

She still couldn't believe that she'd managed to get into that filthy building unnoticed. It certainly hadn't been easy. Recollections of the day before played about her mind as the ladies in the line nearby chatted amiably amongst themselves, ignoring Trudy.

With a swift glance around the area to make sure she wasn't being watched, Trudy had darted between the two buildings and ran toward the door that she knew Marlon Jones kept propped open in the back of his establishment.

She'd prayed that Mathias Sinclair had gotten her message and was already awaiting her inside. Sneaking into the Rotgut Saloon to meet him had been insanity, but she felt it only right to warn the man. If her father found out about what she had done, she would surely suffer for it. So Trudy knew that she had to be careful.

Hesitantly she slid through the door that was left ajar and wrinkled her nose at the smell that permeated the air. The contrasting odors of stale cigarillos, liquor, unwashed bodies, and a hint of something she'd rather not guess the origin, hit her hard. One hand covered her mouth and nose while the other pressed against her stomach in hopes of keeping her food down. Good gracious!

What in the world would possess a man to want to come into such a stench filled den of sin anyway? Trudy shuddered as she glanced around the narrow hallway looking for the door that led into the room that the town council used to conduct their meetings... or so she'd overheard that they did. There was only one door to the left, so that had to be it. Squaring her shoulders, Trudy reached a hand out.

"Heaven help me," she whispered, praying for the strength to follow through.

Before she could turn the grubby knob, the door swung open and Trudy lost her balance. Falling forward she'd yelped, unable to catch her footing.

"Umph..." Trudy muttered as she fell heavily, face first into the broad chest of the very man she'd been seeking.

"You're late," he'd barked out by way of greeting as he'd righted her on her feet.

"I do beg your pardon, I don't happen to have much practice sneaking into these types of establishments," Trudy answered archly as she tucked the book she held under her arm.

"Come in before you're seen," Mathias Sinclair grumbled as he'd swiftly yanked her further into the room and shut the door behind them. "This is no place for a lady to be," he chastised her.

Trudy took a deep breath and was grateful that the interior of the room was not odiferous in the least. In fact, the room was pleasantly filled with a hint of Mathias' heady male fragrance. The spicy scent was quite a delightful change to her previously offended senses, so Trudy took in another delicate whiff in appreciation.

"They had an incident with Dover's pig last night," Mathias remarked as he'd

grabbed a tight hold of her elbow and directed her into taking a seat at the table that was centered within the room.

"Pig?"

"Dover's pig crashed through town last night and got into Marlon's place. That's the smell you were avoiding in the hall," he had explained.

Mr. Sinclair had apparently witnessed her trying to keep her morning meal in her stomach. Trudy nearly groaned aloud in mortification.

"Your note claimed urgency. So, what's this all about?" Mathias demanded.

His large body crowded hers, making it nearly impossible to think. One large palm planted heavily on the table, while his other hand gripped the back of her chair. Trudy sat stupefied staring up at him, at a loss of words.

"Take a seat please," Trudy managed to utter as she indicated the empty chair at the end of the table. She needed space between them, if she was going to be able to put together a coherent thought.

With a loud sigh, Mathias had stomped over and surprisingly did as she'd bid.

Trudy had studied the man seated across from her in the backroom of the smoke filled saloon. His large frame had dwarfed the *small chair that he'd pulled up to the scarred wooden table before facing her. Mathias Sinclair, the man everyone referred to secretly as the 'giant,' was not one to stand on formalities, so he hadn't bothered to even remove his hat. The dark brim was low on his sandy blond head, but it did nothing to block those Steely eyes as they had pierced through her. His square jaw was set in such a manner that Trudy had little doubt of his annoyance with her.*

"Thank you for agreeing to meet with me," Trudy began with a bright smile, hoping to ease the tension in the room.

Mathias had just sat there mutely, sizing her up, and Trudy figured that he probably found her lacking. She wasn't used to the feeling. Men had found Trudy compelling since her first blossom of womanhood. They vied to take her walking or on picnics. They fought over the honor of picking daisies to present to her. She heard countless bad poems dedicated to the cornflower hue of her eyes, or the peachy tone of her complexion. Those men brave enough to compare her lips to berries usually tried to steal kisses and Trudy had even allowed a few of them a brief taste. Judging by the expression that had resided on Mathias

Sinclair's face, he was not in the least impressed by her countenance nor did he look inclined for a kiss. *More's the pity.* Trudy secretly found the man fascinating and she wouldn't have minded a bit more of flirtation from him.

"This isn't a ladies' social," Mathias snapped. "I'm not about to offer you tea cakes, so you might as well go on and clue me in on why we're here, Sugar."

"I'm here to save you. You should be thankful that I've come to you, and not be so rude!" Trudy had exclaimed a tad bit too dramatically. But, in her opinion, dramatics were in order. She had stolen from her parent, walked all the way to the saloon in her new boots that pinched her toes painfully, and risked her spotless reputation. She did not deserve his sarcasm. Who was he to criticize her?

"Well?" Mathias Sinclair prompted her to continue her story as she'd sat glaring at him stonily.

"It's all right here in Papa's ledger. The money your parent's have been depositing is gone... all of it," she had confirmed as she had slid the slim book across the table toward him. "You can check for yourself. The figures don't add up with *those in the ledger that I stole from your parent's shop."*

He did not seem in the least surprised when she'd confessed to the theft and Trudy felt a moment of embarrassment. The large man had been skeptical of her motives of that she could tell, but at least he hadn't disregarded the information up to that point.

"It can't be. Pa would've come to me if they were having money issues," Mathias forcefully denied her claim.

"The mayor has come forward to pay their debt, but I heard Papa telling Mother, that he was still going to find a way to foreclose on your parent's dress shop this week. He had your father sign the shop over to him a while back; he said that the money wouldn't be enough to save them, now that he was the deed…"

Trudy would not go into further detail about what else her father had done. She had revealed enough to the man. Some things she needed to keep close to the vest.

"How can he? If the debt is paid, your father has no leg to stand on," Mathias Sinclair had demanded angrily as he rose from his chair and stood over her. "I am not going to let your father do this to my family!"

"I don't know how he plans to do it, Mr. Sinclair," Trudy had said as she rose from her own seat and had stood toe to toe with him.

She was a tall woman. At seven inches past five foot, she was used to towering over most of the young ladies of her acquaintance, but Mathias Sinclair made her feel as if she were petite. As he had loomed over her, Trudy's head tilted back in order to meet his furious gaze. She would not allow him to cower her.

"I just want you to stop my papa before things get too far out of hand," she assured him.

Trudy still had not the slightest idea as to why her father had held such a powerful dislike of all things Sinclair, but she knew her papa meant to destroy them all. Thomas Bixby was out to destroy the entire town according to the ledgers that she'd found.

"Don't you worry Miss Bixby," Mathias assured her grimly. "I will put a stop to it right now."

"What do you plan to do?" she asked anxiously, only to be ignored.

As Mathias Sinclair had turned on heel and stormed out of the backroom, leaving her to find her own way out of the saloon *undetected, Trudy realized that the man never did answer her. That was when the enormity of what she'd done had sunk in. Trudy was in trouble deep, and it was too late to turn away from it.*

Trudy had gone home from her meeting with Mathias wondering if she'd done the right thing. She was no friend to the Sinclair's, and heaven knew she was not an angel in this scheme, but it was time to figure out what her papa was doing with all of that money. To do that, Trudy needed to confront the man himself. Unfortunately, her papa had spent most of that night in his office with the door barred, so Trudy had been forced to give up and go to bed. In the morning, Thomas Bixby was gone before she'd time to catch him unaware, so Trudy had been forced to march down to his bank to confront him.

"Just what is going on out here?" Thomas demanded as he finally stormed from his office. Exasperated by having his day interrupted by his daughter's presence, he wore a heavy scowl. Trudy shook off thoughts of her meeting with Mathias Sinclair and concentrated on confronting her papa.

"Papa!" Trudy exclaimed. "I need to speak with you."

"*You!*" Thomas Bixby snapped, pointing at the young man standing to Trudy's left, completely ignoring his daughter's distress.

The fine material of his shirt strained against the swell of his hefty stomach. Trudy wondered just how much of her papa's soul he'd had to sell in order to pay for the costume that he wore to disguise just whom he truly was.

"Papa!" Trudy demanded again in impatience. She had not marched all the way down here and torn her pretty dress just to be ignored. She needed to make her father see that what he was doing was wrong.

"You aren't supposed to be here until later in the day," he ranted. "Fools...no one can stick to a plan around here," her father complained in the direction of the young man, once again ignoring his daughter.

"Plan's changed," the irate man snapped back at her father.

"*Papa*?"

Trudy shot a look between the two men. Something was going on that she was not aware of and her hackles rose.

"Shut up!" the dirty man hissed at her angrily.

"I will not! Who are you to be telling me to shut up?" Trudy snapped back.

Trudy couldn't believe saddle- bum- Joe Vernon thought that he could address her in such a way!

"I am the man who is robbing this goddamned bank... that's who!" Joe announced as he pulled a weapon from his coat and brandished it about.

-Woe be to angels that battle bedlam-

CHAPTER TWO

The room was in chaos.

Blood and sweat soaked the bed linens and filled the air with the sharp, nauseating smell of carnage. Rags and bandages littered the ground in pools of crimson. A lantern sitting nearby was the only illumination of the man lying so lifeless on his stomach. The gunshot wound was bad. Located near the lower portion of his spine, the bullet's removal was a daunting task.

He was dying. Right before her very eyes, Mathias Sinclair was fading away. Steeling her resolve, she blotted at the fresh blood and tried to stem the flow. She was not going to let him go, not without a fight.

Gertrude Bixby sighed. She was exhausted and her body ached, but she needed to continue her efforts.

"You can't retrieve all of the fragments Trudy, and you if you keep digging around this close to the spine you're going to do more damage. If we don't close him up, he is going to bleed to death," Sebastian Bixby's hands trembled violently as he turned to his sister. "There's nothing else you could've done."

"It's not fair!"

"Nothing in life is, Trudy," Sebastian whispered sadly, and Trudy was reminded of just how much the mysterious tremors in her brother's hands had started to affect him. The shaking had started randomly last spring, but as months went on now, they became more frequent. Together they'd searched medical tomes, and written many physicians seeking advice for a cure, but nothing they'd tried had worked. The shaking only managed to get worse, until Sebastian, having a hard time hiding the tremors from his patients, had begged Trudy to be his hands for him. Trudy, who'd often gone along with Sebastian on his house calls, had reluctantly agreed. How could she deny him? The fact that she got to learn the art of medicine alongside Sebastian, was an added bonus to being his surreptitious assistant.

The irony of the situation was that Sebastian had always hated the profession that their father had pushed him into. While Trudy, on the other hand would have given her eye teeth to be able to practice medicine. Alas, she would have never been allowed to follow that dream. As her father always reminded her, women were useless and too weak to perform the duties of a man.

Once, Trudy had saved up the courage to beg her papa to send her to the New England Female Medical College in Boston, but her father had absolutely forbidden it. When she had tried to broach the subject, Thomas Bixby had reminded his daughter with the back of his hand, just where her place was. Her mother, never one to go against her husband, had also refused to hear her pleas. The woman had nearly fainted when Trudy first confessed her longing to become a doctor. She'd sworn her daughter was unnatural, warning that she'd lock her in her room, if Trudy so much as breathed her appalling aspiration outside of their home.

Trudy had paid them no mind. Sebastian had always supported her dream though. Patiently teaching her what he could.

As long as her father had not found out what she did, Trudy could do whatever she pleased. It wasn't easy, as Thomas watched his daughter like a hawk, as if waiting for her disobedience, but Trudy managed to keep her involvement a secret. Getting around her mama was much easier, most times she just pretended to go shopping as to avoid arguing with the nagging woman. Too many times she had actually shopped, judging by the balances that she left in her wake at the Sinclair's dress shop. At night, Trudy would just sneak out around to the side of the house where Sab would be waiting in his wagon for her. It was worth the risk, because Sebastian needed her.

If she stuck to only helping her brother with the people on the outskirts of town, no one was the wiser to her activities. The folks they helped rarely came into town anyway, as they were wary of being hassled, and for good reason. As most of Sebastian's patients were nearby sharecroppers, they were no strangers to trouble.

While Liberty was a town filled with somewhat welcoming folk, the neighboring populations of Rattlesnake Canyon, and

Belton City, were brewing beds of hostilities. People didn't take too kindly toward what most considered grubby land grabbers, and a few skirmishes had broken out.

The freed slaves, immigrants, and former soldiers who were considered crippled beyond use, had in the past few years flooded the land. Side by side they worked hoping to obtain a piece of soil for their families. They were poor, but they refused charity. Most times the people traded goods to Sebastian for his help. Other times, they traded services.

Her father had always mocked his son for his charitable works. He'd called him a fool, and warned him away from such practices, but Sebastian had a soft heart. He was so unlike their father who only cared for the gleam of gold or the weight of silver.

"Trudy?" Sebastian prompted his sister as she stood in contemplation.

"Sorry," Trudy mumbled as she set her mind on the task at hand.

Pushing a golden ringlet from her brow using the back of one bloodied hand, Trudy walked over to her brother's side and stared down at the patient. Mathias Sinclair was thankfully unconscious. His large frame dwarfed the dark colored settee he was sprawled upon in the shabby parlor. She was glad he would not feel what came next, although, this would probably the easiest part of the night.

"I will need you to hold the lantern while I thread the needle. Do you think you can, Sab?" Trudy asked the haggard man as she set the fresh bandages down.

"Yes Trudy," Sebastian agreed with a nod, but she could tell that he was already growing green about the gills. His hands had begun their tale tell tremble and Trudy knew that her brother was nearing the end of his endurance.

"Sab, all you have to do is hold the lantern. You can sit while I stitch him up," Trudy said gently. "I know today has been hard for you."

The tragedy had been hard on the both of them. The bank robbery that had left Mathias Sinclair near to death had already cost Trudy and Sebastian's father his life. Her papa had schemed one too many times with the wrong types of people and now so many folks suffered because of it…because of her. She should have stopped it all, but instead she allowed her father's greed to get the better of her. She had helped plan the downfall of innocent people by never speaking up. She'd only wanted to please him, to finally earn her father's respect; instead she'd only blackened her own soul.

Grabbing the materials that she required, Trudy set to work preparing to stitch the man back together. The cut that she'd had to make in order to fish for the bullet was only a few inches in width. It would not take long to repair, but it would be heart breaking. With the sealing of this wound, which was risky enough, he could still contract a fever, infection at the site, blood poisoning… anything. They could still lose him. Taking a deep breath, Trudy steadied her hand and got to work. She could not allow him to die. He was her salvation.

Why in the world had Mathias Sinclair stepped in front of that bullet for her? They were hardly what one would call friends. A few times in the past Trudy had flirted with him, but that was only so that she could help her father with his scheme to bring the Sinclair family to ruins. In the end, she had gone against her father and warned Mathias about her papa's plan. Could he have saved her for that very reason?

"You can come and inspect the sutures now," Trudy informed her brother, wearily minutes later.

The stitches were nice and even. She may not know how to sew a new frock, but she could do one bang up job of knitting flesh back together. With Sebastian's help, together they cleaned and tightly wrapped Mathias Sinclair's muscular torso with fresh linen.

"Trudy, you know that we can never tell anyone what happened tonight, don't you?" Sebastian informed her. "I don't want anyone to blame you for this. It's not your fault, but no one would understand."

"I know," she replied and fought tears.

The thought of Sebastian walking through the parlor doors and telling the family that waited beyond his prognosis hurt her stomach. "How do you tell them that their son will never walk again?" she asked. "What will you say?"

"There are far worse things that I could be telling them right now. I'll just tell them the truth, that the bullet was impossible to fully remove," Sebastian assured her softly.

The family had waited long enough for word on Mathias and the siblings knew it, but neither was looking forward to the telling.

"Maybe the Sinclair family will allow us to clean up before we head home. Mama shouldn't see us covered in blood, and your dress is beyond ruined," Sebastian pondered as she began gathering his instruments.

"Sebastian, I'm not going home," she informed her brother as she returned to her vigil by Mathias' side.

"What? You have to! Someone needs to help get father's body ready for burial," her brother argued. "You know Mother is way too fragile to handle the chore."

"Sebastian, he saved me. I cannot leave Mathias Sinclair. I won't leave him, he needs me," Trudy stated firmly.

"But…but our father!"

"Father made his choices Sebastian. You and I both know the truth about our papa. He would have let me die in that hold up. If it meant that he could keep his money and all his secrets, he would have sacrificed any one of us."

"Trudy! How can you say that about him? It is not like you to be so cold," Sebastian argued hotly.

"Sebastian, you don't understand. I helped Papa create this mess. And, now that he is gone, I am the only one left to clean it up."

"Clean it up? Trudy, what do you have planned?" Sebastian demanded to know.

Trudy sighed tiredly.

"Just go home to Mama, tell her that I will be around to see her. Just as soon as I know all is well here."

"She won't like this one bit," Sebastian warned his sister.

"I know Sab, but Mama loves me. She will understand."

Unfortunately, Trudy was solely relying on hope for that last part.

***

Etta Howard sat huddled in the back of her Uncle Baxter's livery praying that her body would stop its violent shaking. Her stomach felt queasy and though she didn't feel faint, she'd barely made it here to her favorite place, before she'd collapsed in a heap. Finding the place deserted, she'd intended to find solace amongst the horses that she loved so much. The soft nickering usually soothed any hurt that she'd felt, but not today. She was beyond soothing. Etta had watched men die today, and for a moment, thought that she would not see the morrow herself.

Tears burned the lids of her eyes as she squeezed her lashes together trying to stop the flow. She couldn't go into the little house that she shared with her mother. Not yet. Mother would just berate her for not getting the banking done and have their stew on the table by now. Supper time had passed hours ago and yet, here Etta sat reliving the horror that she'd witnessed while her mother was probably wondering what had become of her.

A creaking of the stable door sounded and Etta sucked in a breath. She didn't want to be seen crying like a child in the freshly bedded stall. The light trudging of footsteps over the dirt path between the horse filled stalls signaled that the interloper was near. Etta wished whomever it was would just turn on heel and go away.

"Baxter? You back there?" a man called out and Etta's eyes widened. She knew that voice. It was the very same gravelly timbre which filled her day dreams as she went about her chores. She knew without a doubt who was calling out for her uncle and Etta prayed that he wouldn't peek over the short door that led into her hidey hole.

"Baxter? I've got a hand cart waiting out front if you just want to point me toward the barrel, I'll grab it."

Etta stiffened as the footsteps stopped right outside of the stall she was hiding in.

"Bax? You there?"

Etta, in her effort to make herself as small as possible, scooted her body back into the stall wall. Her foot connected with a plank of wood with a clack. The sound was deafening to her ears and she winced.

"Miss Etta?"

Etta looked up into the scarred face of Tex Brody as he stared down at her in disbelief. Her chin quivered in embarrassment as he studied her as if she were a curious bug scuttling across his shoe.

"Are you alright?" he inquired.

Words lodged in her throat, Etta could only shake her head. She hated that Tex was seeing her like this. The man she'd spent the last few months dreaming of shouldn't witness her at her weakest.

Though she prayed he'd just leave, the man instead entered the stall and walked toward her.

"Why are you sitting all alone in here?" Tex asked as he reached over and turned up the wick of the oil lamp that hung on a peg between the door and entryway. The glow was as unwelcome to her eyes as she was sure her presence must be to him.

"What on earth? There is blood on your dress!" Tex exclaimed as dropped to his knees before her and began checking Etta for trauma. "Miss Etta?" Tex inquired as his large hands skimmed across her bare arm. "What's happened? Where are you hurt?"

"Robbery..." she managed through clattering teeth. "They're dead..."

"You were there? You saw what happened?" Tex asked her grimly.

As she nodded he sighed.

"Damn," he muttered before wincing. "Sorry 'bout the language ma'am," he apologized.

Christopher Brody, otherwise known as 'Tex', hadn't expected to find Miss Etta Howard sitting in the near darkness of her uncle's livery. He'd only come to purchase a barrel of stearin that the man had been fermenting for him. Finding Etta had been much more interesting than purchasing animal fat for his candle shop, but he'd certainly not wanted to see the sweet woman in such a condition. His heart had nearly exploded when he'd saw the blood on the bodice of her gown. For a once convicted murderer such as he, Tex shouldn't have felt the utter panic that he had. He'd seen and done a hell of a lot worse, he was used to bloodshed. But this woman was an innocent lamb; she didn't deserve to know what a cesspit the world actually was.

"Why don't we get you home ma'am?" he offered gently. As Etta shook her head once again in obvious objection, Tex decided he'd better take a seat. The tiny woman wasn't going to be going anywhere for a while, and neither would he. Tex would just have to wait her out.

Together they sat in silence until finally sobs burst from the woman at his side. It was a good sign, her weeping. It meant that she was finally coming out of her shock.

"Cry it on out ma'am," Tex encouraged as he reached into his vest pocket for a clean handkerchief. "Sometimes it's worse if you try to keep it in," he murmured as he pressed the cloth into her small hand.

Tex wanted to pull her into his lap and rock her like a child but decided that would be foolhardy. The woman would think he'd lost all his wits had he tried, and he didn't want to scare her any more than she already was.

After a few moments, Etta finally wiped her eyes one last time, and tucked the plain square of linen into the sleeve of her dress. Though he shouldn't have done it, for it certainly wasn't proper, Tex took her hands in his and rubbed her icy fingers between his own. "When you're ready, you just take my arm, and I'll see you home," he offered as he tried his best to warm her.

"Thank you," Etta murmured softly. "I best get on home. Mother will be worried."

"I reckon she probably is," Tex agreed.

Placing her hand on the crook of his elbow, Etta allowed Tex to assist her to her feet.

It was a short walk to her home just down the narrow lane, but he was determined to see Etta to her stoop. He didn't know quite what to say to the woman without sounding like a buffoon, so he walked mutely by her side. All the while they slowly strolled, he wanted to kick himself. This was his chance to finally talk to her and he couldn't get past the lump in his throat.

At the door, Tex tipped his hat, and screwed up his courage. "I'm looking forward to our courting nights," he admitted gruffly. "When all this madness settles down and the council boys decide to reinstate the courtship rules, that is."

"I—"

The door swung open before Etta could say what was on her mind. A furious matron of middling years and heavy of gut stood glaring angrily at him. Her lip curled into a sneer as she noticed that Tex still had one hand on Etta's arm.

"Etta!" she snapped, reaching one hand out and grabbing her daughter by the arm. "You get yourself in this house this instant!"

Before Tex could blink, the woman dragged her daughter through the entryway and slammed the door in his face; leaving him slack jawed on the stoop.

Not a good sign, he thought with a groan. When it came to courting, an angry mother was a dangerous obstacle.

***

Edna Bixby sat alone in the front parlor of the grand home that she'd shared with her husband. As she stared at the spot where his body lay so still and pale, awaiting burial, she only felt emptiness.

Pots of boiled herbs simmered throughout the house, in hopes of keeping the room from smelling of death. Flowers had been all but impossible to find after the last snowfall, so no wreath was hung to aid in the cause. The few precious summer sachets that the maids had made for Edna's linen closet would have to do. The lavender and clove packets adorning Thomas' chest were not even made of the finest lace, but simple cheesecloth. A sad tribute for a man as important as he, and Edna felt tears well in her eyes.

After tomorrow they would lay him in the ground, and her world would never be the same. No longer a wife, with no children left to raise, what would she do with herself? For twenty nine years she'd loved a man that hadn't returned even an ounce of the sentiment. Though he'd pledged to love her until his dying day, Edna knew that Thomas' heart had never really managed to allow her in, even as he lay bleeding to death on his bank floor, his only true love stolen from him, she bet he hadn't thought of her. Money was his one true mistress, and Edna had never been able to compete with it.

While Thomas had only lived for his wealth, she lived for him.

Her lips quivered and Edna pressed them into a grim line, refusing to allow the weakness. She couldn't afford to break right now; she was all she had left and needed to be strong. Sebastian, her son, was trying to help, that much was true, but one day he'd leave her alone just as everyone else had... just as her ungrateful daughter had done. She would be alone and unloved.

Rising from the settee, Edna walked toward her husband's body intending to adjust the lapels of his finest coat. It wouldn't do for him to be buried looking unkempt.

So many years, so little she really knew of the man lying there. She couldn't help but think back on how her life had changed because of this man.

Once long ago, Edna had been beautiful and adored. The eldest daughter of Clive and Gabriela Despre, wealthy merchants, Edna had been spoiled and cherished. Life in New Orleans had been exciting and she'd felt the bayou in her creole blood. Oh, the parties, the dances, and the picnics she'd taken part in! Edna had never once considered anything beyond her reach. The man who'd waltz into her life in the sixteenth year of her life had changed all of that.

So many suitors had vied for her hand in those days, but she'd only wanted one. Thomas. So young, so handsome, he'd certainly not been the plump and pampered shell that his body had become.

Orphaned Thomas had grown up in a foundling home in Natchez and somehow made his way to La Nouvelle-Orléans, hoping for a better life. He hadn't much to recommend him, but Edna's papa had taken a chance and hired the young man.

Poor and looked down upon by his peers, Thomas had managed to acquire a manager's position in her father's company. Edna remembered how Thomas had struggled to find acceptance amongst the other young men that her father employed, but none wanted him. They saw him as someone without worth.

Edna, who'd grown up playing amongst the warehouses and shipyards, much to her mother's complaints, spent much of her time following her father around. She had taken one glance at him and fallen in love. He was so sullen, so brooding, that something about him had called to her. She'd longed to bring a smile to his handsome face.

Thomas in return, had taken one look at her and knew that she was his ticket to a better life. Oh, she knew that he'd only married her for her fortune, but she'd wanted him so badly that she hadn't cared. By the end of her seventeenth year, they were married and he was made a partner in her father's business. Her papa had wanted his new son by marriage close and his daughter well taken care of. It had seemed that their lives were going to be perfect together.

In the end, Edna had only disappointed him. Her father's business had fallen to ruins after their deaths three years later, and Thomas had so much responsibility thrust upon him. Edna's young sister Estella, only thirteen at the time, had come to live with them, further burdening Thomas. He'd been forced to seek work as a clerk in a nearby bank just to put food in their mouths.

Their home and carriages stripped from them, they'd been reduced to renting a set of rooms above a hat shop, barely big enough for the three of them. Gone were her beautiful dresses and jewels, but she didn't care. Edna had only cared that it had hurt Thomas so much to fall back into his previous poverty. She remembered how he'd worn badly hemmed trousers and the same faded overcoat, but he'd sported them like a king. Edna knew that it killed him inside to appear so poor, but Thomas had struggled on.

When it became clear that they couldn't afford to continue caring for Estella, they'd been forced to give her over to Edna's uncle Bernard. She had cried bitterly, but Thomas had sworn it would be temporary. It was either him or her sister, he stated. They could no longer feed the growing girl and if Edna wanted, she could go as well to her uncle's. She'd chosen to kiss Estella goodbye and stay with her husband, to prove her loyalty. Thomas had never thanked her for it. Instead, he'd become cruel and distant with Edna.

For many years she'd been barren and had thought that it was the Lord's way of punishing her for her decision, until a miracle had occurred. After birthing her beautiful Sebastian, Edna had thought that Thomas would finally come to love her and turn his focus unto their new family, but it wasn't to be. He'd already turned to other women and wine to soothe his needs. A year later Gertrude had come along, and although Thomas had taken an interest in having a son, it hadn't lasted long. By the mark of Sebastian's first year, he'd gone back to his ways.

Luck finally rolled the Bixby's way a few years later. Thomas had managed to work his way up into a manager's position in the bank, and the rest seemed to follow suit. Within another five years, her husband had saved enough to move his family westward.

Landing in the small settlement of Liberty, Thomas' dream of opening his own bank had finally come to fruition, and he'd seemed happy. Once again money and a lavish lifestyle were in store for the Bixby family, and her husband made sure that they'd flaunted it. His new dream now that he'd acquired his wealth was power. Thomas wanted nothing more than to gain a position on the council. He saw it as his ticket to ruling his own kingdom. But they'd never accepted him.

As she looked about the opulent formal room with all the materials of wealth, Edna couldn't help but feel sorry for her husband. No matter how rich Thomas became, he'd never found a way to belong. He'd always remained the outsider looking in.

But soon, soon it would all be gone. Just as before, Edna would be without. Except this time, there was no Thomas to see her through it. No, he was dead and would soon be in the cold ground.

Resentment filled Edna's gut as her fists tightened.

It was all because of that Mathias Sinclair. If he hadn't fired Joe Vernon from his ranch all those months ago, the fool wouldn't have been robbing the bank. Not only did Mathias take the man Edna loved, but he'd stolen her daughter from her as well. Trudy never would've dared to dishonor her father the way she had if it weren't for him showing up at the bank that day.

"He'll pay," she managed through clenched teeth. "They'll all pay."

Edna was determined that everyone in town would rue the day they'd crossed her beloved. She owed Thomas that much.

***

The sharp crack of a bullet blasted scant moments before tortured screams filled the room. The sounds echoed, permeating her skull, and ran shivers up her spine.

"Papa!" she gasped.

"Trudy…"

In horror, she watched as her father fell to the ground, a large gaping wound in his middle. She knew without a doubt, that the rupture to his abdomen was a mortal wound and he had only minutes to live.

Scarlet essence seeped forth spreading a stain about the snow white of his shirt. She whimpered as her father struggled to crawl closer to her.

He stretched a bloodied hand outward, in her direction and begged for her help through pale lips, but the sound that came from him was a mere gurgle. Trudy tried to kneel next to him, only to find her legs immobilized with fear.

Panic gripped her, as she realized that she was powerless to save him. She couldn't bear to watch him take his last breath.

Trudy raised her hands to her face in hopes of shielding her eyes to the carnage but found her fingers frozen around the stock of a pistol. As blood dripped from her palms, tendrils of smoke wafted from the barrel. She tried to drop the weapon, only to find it fused to her flesh.

"You did this!" her father cried out as he grasped her ankle roughly. "I'm dying for your cowardice."

"No Papa," she tried to deny.

"You've disappointed me Gertrude."

Trudy tried to back away from her father's reach only to find her footing slip. She screamed as she fell and hit the floor.

"I'm sorry Papa," she begged with a shriek, as she felt her legs start to tug toward his bleeding form. "Let me go!" she sobbed.

She didn't want this; she never wanted any of this to happen.

"It's too late to run; you'll die with me girl," he gargled in response. "You've made your choice...It's your fault. You did this!"

Trudy woke from the nightmare with a cry and reared back. She groaned as her head hit the wooden back of the squat chair that she'd pulled up next to the bed. She'd planned to watch over the unconscious man, but had obviously fallen asleep instead. A miracle, considering the blasted chair was the most uncomfortable thing she'd ever had the misfortune of sitting in.

Rising, she moaned as pain lanced through her posterior. It was all Trudy could do to keep herself from rubbing her aching bottom as she walked toward a small window to the left of the bed. Ladies didn't rub their personal bits in the presence of men, even if said men were passed out cold and probably couldn't care less as to her actions. It just wasn't done, but lord almighty, she so very much wanted to.

Casting a glance through the glass pane, Trudy watched as a single snowflake drifted downward and affixed itself to the wooden frame of the window. Judging by the still darkness the witching hour was upon them, so she hadn't been asleep for long.

Her hands shook slightly as she pulled at the worn bodice of her gown. The nightmare had felt so real that her stomach heaved. The words 'you've made your choice' floated about her mind as tears formed in her eyes. She had. In more ways than one, Trudy had made her choices, she just didn't know if she'd made the right ones.

She'd only meant to confront her father. Trudy never would've guessed that that the man would die in her arms, anger between them.

Only fourteen hours previous, her father had been alive and Mathias Sinclair had been hale and hearty. What an alteration those hours had made in the lives of the folks that had been present in the bank.

"Foolish man, you should have saved your valor for a more deserving woman," Trudy whispered around a sob.

While she was grateful for Mathias' actions, she still felt as if it were his fault that he'd wound up with a bullet for his troubles. He should have let the slug strike her. At least then, the shot would have met a fitting mark. Now, all she could do was hope to right the wrongs that she'd helped her father commit against the wounded man. No matter the cost.

Turning to the bed, Trudy placed a palm against Mathias' handsome cheek and drew her hand back in horror. There may not be time for her to amend her trespasses.

Fever had set in.

Foolish hearts lead to the greatest of
destinations

CHAPTER THREE

Trudy sat silently and watched over the man who had saved her life, as he fought to hang on to his own. The rise and fall of his chest as he struggled for breath worried her. The fever was back again, and she had spent most of the day bathing his brow and upper chest, in effort to cool him off.

For three days now Mathias' body had fought off the hands of death. In his delirium he had yelled, laughed, and lashed out. He had confused her with his late grandmother, his sister, and once even Reverend Peterson. He held conversations with shadows and mumbled threats as his arms thrashed about. His legs remained still, confirming the diagnosis. Trudy was exhausted, but she refused to allow anyone else to care for him.

Charlotte had sat up with Trudy for most of the first night. But she was needed to care for George, her husband, who had been ill for quite some time. Torn between the two men, Trudy had taken the decision out of her tired hands and barred Charlotte Sinclair from the room in the evenings. Mathias' sister, Serena had also come and tried to help. But after Mathias had knocked her to the ground in his struggles, Serena's husband Alec had called a stop to her assistance. Serena's pregnancy was a concern. Mathias could accidentally hurt the babe growing inside of his sister. Serena was now only allowed as far as the doorway when she visited her brother.

Trudy could tell that the other woman was not trusting in her abilities to heal and wanted to take over Mathias' care herself. Not surprising, as Trudy had built up the reputation as a spoiled, selfish, fickle woman. But it still chafed Trudy's pride to be doubted. Grudgingly, Serena had thanked Trudy for caring for Mathias and took her leave, leaving Trudy alone with the deathly pallid man.

The wind howled fiercely, rattling the shutters on the window to the small room. The last few nights had been colder than usual, so Trudy had sat wrapped in a blanket over her borrowed night rail. She would have loved to have had possession of her thick winter robe. Unfortunately, her mother had refused to allow her any of her possessions. After she had refused to return home with her, Trudy's mother had disowned her.

Edna Bixby couldn't understand why her daughter wouldn't help prepare her own father for burial. She was angry that her child had chosen instead to sit by this stranger's bedside, nursing him. As if Mathias Sinclair had more right to life than a wealthy banker had!

Trudy couldn't tell her mother the truth of how her father had brought this all on himself. The very reason Trudy had stormed into the bank to begin with that day, would have to be kept quiet if her mother wanted to continue to hold her head up high in society. Trudy had stolen Thomas Bixby's personal journals that day planning on confronting her father with the evidence that she had found and learned more than she'd wished about the man who'd spawned her.

It would devastate her mother to know what her husband had been planning, and just he had been funding with his ill-gotten gains. If the truth ever got out, the Bixby's would be run out of town faster than a rabid coyote in winter. They would be considered traitors... and traitors could be hanged.

"Mother, he needs me. He saved my life... I can't just leave him," Trudy had argued with the livid woman.

"It should have been you that died instead of your father! You ungrateful beast," Edna Bixby had screamed as she slapped Trudy hard across the cheek. The sting had been so sharp that it had brought tears to Trudy's eyes, and left a large crimson welt on her skin. Trudy had just stood there in her bloody dress, holding the side of her face in shock.

The last she'd seen of her mother was just the woman's back, as Edna had slammed out of the Sinclair's home in fury. Trudy hadn't bothered to weep. She was too tired to even care that she had earned her mother's scorn. It really hadn't been anything new anyway. Her mother had always found fault in her no matter how hard Trudy had tried to please her. Sebastian was Edna's pride and joy, and he'd always be. Her mother had barely tolerated her youngest child.

Mrs. Sinclair had rushed in and tried to comfort Trudy, after her mother had stormed off, but there was not much that she could say. How did one comfort a selfish girl who was barred from attending her own father's funeral? Instead, the kind woman had prepared Trudy a bath in an adjoining room and loaned her one of her daughter's night rails. As tired as Charlotte Sinclair was, she had sat up with Trudy.

Brushing the tangles from her hair, Charlotte pretended that she didn't see the tears that Trudy had brushed from her pale cheeks.

As angry as Trudy had been with her papa, and no matter what his faults, she had still loved the man and felt his loss. Now, she had lost her mother as well.

"Nnnoo," Mathias moaned from the bed drawing Trudy's attention from her personal troubles. He once again back to battering about and she knew that it would only get worse from there. If she did not stop him, he would pull out her stitches again.

Trudy ran over to the bed and tried to calm him with soothing words. She picked up the damp cloth that she had been using to bathe him, and placed it over Mathias' forehead.

"Don't leave me," he whispered weakly, and her heart ached at the anguish she heard in those words.

"No, I won't leave you I promise," she murmured.

Trudy tenderly touched a hand to his jaw. The bristles of hair chaffed her skin, but she was afraid to shave him with the way he thrashed about. She was trying to save him, not cut his throat.

"Kiss me," he begged, and to her surprise he drew her down to him. His arms wrapped around her waist dragging her close to his naked chest.

"Stop Mathias, you will hurt yourself," Trudy admonished gently as she tried to wrest herself from his grip.

"One kiss. Just one, then I will let you go," he muttered. His eyes half opened and glazed, stared into hers. Trudy could not decline a dying man's wish.

"One kiss, Mathias. Just one," she whispered to him before she could help herself.

Leaning her face into his, she pressed her lips against his. Gently, without much pressure, she allowed the press of his firm lips against hers for a brief moment before attempting to pull away.

"You must let me go now," She said as she grazed his cheek with another press of her lips. "I can't let you hurt yourself."

"I love you," he grumbled and Trudy's heart stood still, her breath hitched.

"*What*?" she gasped. "What did you just say Mathias?"

"I love you…"

"You do?" Trudy bit her lip, unsure.

"God damn you Daisy Lynn! I won't beg you again… stay with me. I built the house that you wanted. I can give you everything if you will just let me."

Trudy gulped as tears formed in her eyes. Mathias was lost in his memories of the past. Of course he had no interest in her. How could he? They may have flirted in passing a few times, but his heart had always belonged to that jade Daisy Lynn. Everyone in town had gossiped about how Mathias had closed himself off after the foolish young woman had run back east and found herself a well-to-do fella. She felt silly for even thinking the declaration could have been aimed at her.

"Yes, Mathias… I will stay with you," Trudy whispered in his ear to calm him. Her heart ached, and she smiled ruefully. She had no other option but to stay, she had nowhere else to go now. She was as poor as a church mouse and just as unwanted.

Trudy shook her pale head ruefully. She should have known that he was not dreaming of her. She'd done too many bad things in her life, hurt too many people. No, Trudy accepted that she would never be worthy of a good man's love. In that moment, she had never hated another woman more than she hated Daisy Lynn Howard.

***

Bright sunlight filtered in through the window, waking Mathias Sinclair. His mind felt foggy and his head ached as he looked about the room. Sparse, faded walls, washed in milk paint stared back him, as lace curtains that had seen better days offered no protection from the sun's rays. He blinked as the beams burned into his bleary eyes. The surroundings were as familiar to him as his own name. He was in his old room in his parents' house. A faded quilt was bunched about his hips, and Mathias knew without a doubt that he was naked beneath.

With a groan, he raised a shaky hand and touched his torso. There was a thick linen bandage wrapped tightly around him, and he felt as if it were cutting off his air. Mathias tried to wrest it from him, but found he was too drained to struggle against the confines.

A soft sigh to the right of him drew his attention. As Mathias swiveled his head in the direction of the sound, he was flabbergasted. A woman in a faded, white nightdress was slumped in a sitting position at his side. She snuffled a low snore in her sleep. Her long, pale hair hung over her face obscuring his view, yet he knew her at first glance. Those flaxen tresses of hers were a dead giveaway as to her identity. No other woman in town had hair as fair. His gaze assessed the full length of her form. Nor he decided, had any other woman legs so long.

The Bixby girl.

He knew who slept at his side, what he did not know was how she came to be there, or why.

What in the devil was going on? The last thing he recalled was the bank robbery.

Mathias, with his brother in law Alec in tow, had planned to stomp into the bank and beat Thomas Bixby soundly. The bastard had been stealing from his family and Mathias wanted to know why. Alec Wentworth, who happened to be the mayor of Liberty, had some questions of his own to pose to the man who'd been blackmailing him as well. The two had argued over it, but Mathias had won and was going to get to throw the first punch.

Upon arriving at the bank, their plans had gone bust. Mathias had never dreamt that they would walk into the spectacle that they had.

The sound of weeping women and the stench of black powder assaulted their senses as the men entered the bank. Stepping over the body of the dead teller blocking the doorway, they had surveyed the situation. Another body lay on the polished floor only feet away. The banker would never get his deserved punch in the nose, it seemed, the robber had gotten him first, and there was no satisfaction in beating up a corpse.

Footsteps and the scuffling of something being drug across the floor sounded as Mathias drew his weapon preparing for trouble. The sight of the gun trained on the temple of the banker's daughter had stopped him cold.

Too her credit, Trudy Bixby hadn't looked frightened, merely furious. There was a flash of annoyance in her cornflower eyes and for a moment, Mathias almost felt as if the emotion were directed toward him, instead of the man holding her by the vicious twist of her curls.

Mathias recalled ordering the fool to drop his weapon as Alec moved the other women present out of harm's way.

Either tired of having her hair pulled, or sick of waiting for Mathias to intervene, Miss Bixby decided to take matters into her own hands and fight back.

There was a struggle between the pair as the girl reached up and raked her nails down her captor's face. As the bastard howled in rage, she'd managed to free herself. Running, the woman had nearly made it to the door before the blast sounded.

Mathias remembered running to push Trudy Bixby out of range of the shot, but what happened next was a mystery to him. He certainly didn't remember taking her home to his parents' house and joining her in bed. Not that the thought of bedding her hadn't crossed his mind a time or two in the last few months, but Trudy Bixby was a respectable lady. He would never have crossed the line with the girl. Her reputation would be tarnished, even if he hadn't laid a hand on her. Decent ladies did not sleep in the beds of men they weren't married to. And Mathias knew, without a doubt, that he had not touched the woman, for that was something that he could never have erased from his mind. Making love to the beautiful, haughty, Trudy Bixby would have burned its memory into his soul. Of that, he had no doubt.

Something wasn't right about this. Her parents should be shouting down the house looking for their girl. Mathias knew that he needed to get her out of there and fast, but first he needed to put on some pants before the girl got a glimpse of his greater glory for all it was worth.

Mathias tried to rise up in the bed, but found he couldn't budge. He frowned as he tried once again. The action resulting in failure, only managed to rouse the sleeping woman, who yawned and stretched her arms outward. The act pulled the faded nightdress she wore tight across the swell of her breasts and he could see the outline of the tightened tips of her nipples through the threadbare material. Mathias reluctantly tore his eyes from the enchanting sight and cleared his throat.

Turning at the sound to stare down at him, her mouth hung open in surprise as she caught him gawking up at her.

"You're awake!" she cried out happily with a quick clap of her hands as if he too should be excited for the fact.

"I am not so sure of that. Maybe this is a dream?" Mathias whispered as he narrowed his eyes, observing her. "A beautiful woman in my bed… maybe I should just keep on dreaming?"

"Are you trifling with me again, Mr. Sinclair?" she asked sassily, but he could hear relief in her voice and he wondered at it.

It was her way to flirt, he knew that, but her toying always seemed to get to him. It made him wonder just how far that flirting could go without consequence. Many times of late he found himself tempted to press his lips against the plumpness of hers. Thankfully he'd never taken the opportunity. He tried not to make too many trips into town, for fear that his resolve would weaken and he'd follow through.

Trudy smiled down at him, and for a brief moment, Mathias felt like grinning right back at her, until pain lanced through him once again and he found himself groaning instead.

"What's going on?" Mathias croaked out. His throat felt raw and he winced as his head began to pound.

"Let me get you some water," she offered as she slipped from the bed and poured water from a pitcher into the small tin cup that sat beside it. "Here. Drink this, you will feel much better."

Mathias took a substantial sip of the tepid liquid before pushing away the offered cup.

"What are you doing in my room?" Mathias asked the burning question on his mind.

"Oh." She looked at him blankly before clearing her throat and continuing on. "I came to check on you in the middle of the night. You were restless, and I was afraid that you may injure yourself further, so I stayed." Shrugging as if finding herself awakened in a stranger's bed was no rarity, Trudy smiled. "I must've fallen asleep."

"What happened? I remember the holdup at the bank," Mathias began. "I recall hearing a gunshot. Was Serena hurt?" he asked worried for his sister who'd been present in the depository that day.

"Joe Vernon was the one robbing the bank. My father and the clerk were killed and Joe got away," she informed Mathias solemnly. "Serena was unharmed."

"I'm sorry for your loss Miss Bixby," Mathias murmured. Thomas Bixby was a thief as far as Mathias was concerned, but the man was still her father, and a lady, out of respect, was due condolences.

"Thank you," Trudy replied softly.

He wondered if he should do something for her, maybe pat her hand, but Mathias thought the better of it. Displays of emotion always made him feel awkward, and he worried she might burst into tears if he did. He'd rather swallow lamp oil than listen to a lady cry.

Clearing his throat, Mathias once again asked, "Why are you here?"

"You were hurt saving me. It's been four days since you were shot," she explained patiently.

"*Shot?*" Mathias echoed numbly, but the memory was becoming clearer. He remembered the jolt of the bullet as it had slammed into him, a searing pain that had spread through his legs, and then nothing more.

"Unfortunately you turned feverish," she explained. "I've been looking after you."

"You've been looking after me?" he asked her skeptically. "What was your brother thinking, allowing you to stay?"

"I gave him no choice in the matter," she stated firmly with a defiant toss of her moonlight curls.

Trudy's brother, Sebastian though young, was a decent sort and a competent doctor, but he was one piss poor brother if he'd left his sister to care for a naked man, unconscious or not. Mathias would never have allowed his sister to do so. But then again, Serena had always done just whatever she wanted.

Not too long ago Mathias had been forced to coerce his own friend Alec, at the point of his gun, into becoming Serena's husband, due to an incident that Mathias wished would fade from his memory. His gut churned as thoughts of walking in on the pair resurfaced. The sight of the two naked and intertwined had burned his eyes and if he lived a hundred years, he'd never forgive his friend for seducing his sister. Serena, who'd been angry at Mathias for having the good sense to intervene, had stomped her little foot. She'd cursed him for trying to care for her as any brother would. So, if Trudy Bixby were as headstrong as his sister, then Mathias felt pure sympathy for the young man she called brother.

"Does your head pain you?"

"A bit," he admitted.

"You fell on top of me and hit your head on the corner of the door," she explained when his hands went to investigate the bandage on the side of his skull near the temple. "It was the least of your injuries, but it may be the reason you're having a hard time remembering what occurred."

"I think it's all starting to come back to me. So if you'll pardon me Darlin', I think I'll get dressed and go see what is being done to catch the vermin that did this."

"Mathias you can't—"

"You should get going before someone catches you in my room dressed like that," he said with a smirk. "Not that I'm complainin' or nothin', but I think some folks would have a problem with it."

"Mathias, you need to listen to me—"

"Suit yourself lady, but I got things to do. Don't blame me if you catch an eyeful."

Throwing back the covers, Mathias tried to rise and leave the bed. He frowned as his legs refused to cooperate with the rest of him. Trying to turn his body onto his side, he struggled to pull himself into a sitting position, but failed. In shock, he realized that he could not move his lower extremities even the slightest bit.

"Mathias please—"

With a grunt, Mathias labored again. He put all of his weight into the action this time, rocking his upper body violently. Instead of gaining his footing as he'd expected, he found himself face first in a heap on the ground. Agonizing pain reverberated through him. Exposing his body to her was the least of his issues; Mathias had the misfortune of learning.

As Trudy began to shout out for help, Mathias gritted his teeth against the pain and rolled himself until his back was against the wooden slats of bed. Grunting, he used the muscles of his upper body to pull himself into a sitting position. Agony clawed at his back as Mathias tried and once again and failed to lift his body onto the side of the bed. He strained and struggled, but continued to collapse to the floor. He could feel his legs, but why couldn't he use them?

"Mathias, please stop! You're going to hurt yourself," Trudy begged him, but he had no time for her warnings.

Something was wrong, but he couldn't process what exactly was going on. Fear clenched at his gut. This couldn't be happening… this had to be a dream. He would wake up, and find that he had imagined this.

"You can't walk!" she cried out, disillusioning him. "You may never walk again!"

"You're lying," he accused her as he grasped for a better hold on the bedding and pulled himself up higher.

"No, I swear it. Sebastian had Dr. Fisher exam you as well, and they both agreed. Your mother has already wired for an ambulatory chair. She expects it will be delivered within a month."

Ignoring her chattering, he continued on with his struggles. One hand wrapped around the bed post, Mathias heaved with all of his strength. He'd nearly succeeded in lifting up to the ridges of his ribs over the top of the bed, when Trudy dropped to her knees before him, wanting to assist. Her arms wrapped around his waist, even as he ordered her to release him. She had no business near his naked groin, and Mathias didn't want her help. He was going to get back up on that bed without anyone's help.

Ignoring his grumbling, Trudy tried to push him higher. Unfortunately, her gown chose that moment to become tangled about her legs, causing her to fall heavily into his torso. Trying to right herself, the woman pulled swiftly backward. The momentum brought the already weak Mathias crashing back to the floor, this time atop her. His groin cushioned against her breasts as her face was pressed awkwardly against his navel.

"Sweet Jesus!" Mathias hissed as he realized that her hands were clawing at his bare bottom and he couldn't feel a blasted thing. She was obviously trying to push him off of her and he had no strength left to help.

Footsteps sounded outside the door just as Trudy began thrashing about in earnest, the hem of her gown rose high above her knees as she kicked furiously.

His mother, alarmed by Trudy's previous cries, stormed into the room to find him bare-assed, draped across Trudy like a second skin and shrieked to the heavens, as if she'd found the room on fire. The bedding slipped from his grasp, as Mathias stared up at the door with horror.

"Dear lord!" Charlotte Sinclair exclaimed, rushing to kneel beside the pair. "Mathias, what are you doing to the poor girl?" she demanded.

"Really, Mother?" Mathias huffed as the older woman began yanking on his upper arms trying in vain to untangle the pair. "Does this look like something enjoyable for me?"

"Matt," his mother wheezed. "You don't want to know what this looks like to me. This is indecent, to say the very least."

"Just help me off of her," Mathias blustered. Short all of Trudy's thrashing and muffled shouts, and in any other circumstance, finding himself in this position would have been the stuff of dreams. Sadly, he was in too much pain to appreciate the irony.

With effort, Charlotte managed to help her son push his body from Trudy's, before quickly grabbing the rumpled sheet from the bed and covering him with it.

As Mathias lay on the ground next to a panting Trudy, Charlotte rose to her feet and went to the door intending on summoning the young Doctor Bixby.

"Trudy my dear," Charlotte called out in warning, "It may be best if your brother didn't find you in your nightclothes when he arrives."

Trudy released a delicate cough as the door closed behind his mother.

Mathias turned his head in her direction and watched as the girl slowly recovered her breath. He, himself, was at a loss for words. Confusion and denial swirled within his brain. Fear boiled in his belly.

"You should have just listened to me," she managed weakly.

"Son of a bitch," he moaned.

And so began the nightmare from which he couldn't awaken.

-Careful the poison a vipers tongue
holds-

CHAPTER FOUR

"I hear that she is living in sin with the man!" A scandalized whisper announced to the room of ladies gathered. "Pretty as you please, she just up and moved in with Mathias Sinclair."

It was Tuesday, and as tradition, the sewing circle was meeting and local gossip was flying. This week the honor of hosting was bestowed unto the O'Malley family ranch. The Lucky M was a good hour's ride from town, so the meeting would blissfully be a short one. The head of the house, Gabriel, no doubt had the good sense to hide himself in his barn until the petticoat flock took their leave.

"It's true. I watched the wagon carrying them both, drive out of town that day. I could only wonder what Charlotte Sinclair was thinking to allow that girl to accompany her son," a second voice confirmed.

The room was becoming overly warm and a few of the ladies present fanned themselves off lazily with their hands. The weather was still a bit cool as winter came to an end, but Florrie Pritchard was filled to the seams with hot air, and the horrid gossip was determined to spill it all, causing the room to become stifling.

"Oh hush!" Winifred Lawrence snapped at the gray haired gossip. "Idle tongues are the devil's handiwork." Crossing her arms over her ample bosom, Winnie glared at the reed thin woman seated across from her.

"That's idle hands," Melody O'Malley gently corrected her elderly friend as she rocked her newborn daughter in her arms.

"Tongues, hands…it's all the same," Winnie said with a shrug.

"Well, it's just not right," Florrie insisted as she picked up another square of ivory material to sew for her portion of the quilt. "That girl is no better than she should be."

"Fine talk coming from a lady whose pa had to march her own groom down the aisle with a loaded shotgun at his back," Winnie snapped.

"He did no such thing Winnie Lawrence!" Florrie cried out.

"If I remember correctly, your oldest boy came a good three months earlier than the required nine. Hm?" Winnie announced slyly.

"You leave Baylor out of this! He was born early that's all."

"The boy was at least ten pounds. Florrie, sell your manure to someone else," Winnie announced with a smirk. "All of us here know exactly what you were up to all those years ago."

"Baylor was a healthy eater," Florrie countered red faced. "And speaking of indecency, don't you go thinking that I don't know all about you and Fergus O'Malley stepping out, Winnie Lawrence."

"And, just what is that supposed to mean?" Winnie demanded.

"Don't think that everybody here doesn't know that you and that old fool are 'sparkin' on your 'walks'… as if a man with gout goes out for a stroll!"

The ladies in the room gasped as Winnie said a word that curled their graying hair.

"Oh gracious!" one of the ladies straining to hear the argument cried out. "Did Winnie Lawrence really say what I think she said?"

"I'm half deaf and even I heard her!" another remarked, scandalized.

"There is nothing going on between me and that old goat O'Malley!" Winnie snapped furiously ignoring the chatter about her.

"Nothing?" Florrie scoffed. "Well my Harold was at the Rotgut Saloon last week to deliver some of my pickled vegetables, mind you," Florrie said with a sly grin. "And he said that Fergus was looking mighty proud of himself. He was all spiffed up, so Harold asked him why, and he said that he was going to see a certain lady regarding some business."

"Well it wasn't me, and I thank you to mind your own business. And that goes double for your nosy husband Harold, as well!"

"Ladies, please, let's not argue," Melody pleaded. "We are all supposed to be working together."

As the youngest member of the sewing circle and the most even tempered of those present, Melody tried to be the voice of reason. Lifting the babe onto her shoulder, she patted her tiny back gently, as she frowned at the four other ladies in her sitting room. "What goes on at the Bar S is none of our concern," she chided Florrie.

"It's just not Christian," Florrie muttered in defense as she shot a sour look at Mrs. Lawrence.

Turning to a smug Winnie Lawrence, Melody addressed her as well. "Winnie, apologize to Florrie for what you called her," she ordered.

"I will certainly not!" Winnie cried out.

"You will, if you ever want to hold little Moira Elizabeth again," Melody coerced.

"I'm sorry," Winnie mumbled irritably. "But you know how I feel about anyone talking about Mathias Sinclair. He's a good boy, and it's a tragedy about what's happened to him."

"It's not him that I am talking about. It's that no good Bixby girl that has gone and done him in. She's the one who needs to be punished," Florrie said evenly. "We all know how she turned her back on her own mama after her pa was killed. Now I ask you, what kind of daughter does that?"

"Mrs. Pritchard, we don't know what really happened," Melody broke in. "As far as I'd heard, Trudy was asked not to attend her own father's funeral. What kind of a mother does that?"

"You'll learn with your own little one, Melody. Sometimes daughters just need a firm hand. In this case, that Bixby girl needs a firm hand across her bottom quarters!" Florrie declared hotly. "Living it up like a heathen, while the rest of us good folk look on in shock, for shame!"

"Something tells me that Trudy Bixby isn't so happy with her new surroundings," Alice Monroe confided. Alice, not one to usually voice her opinion, obviously felt that now was the time to add fire to the flames. "I saw her in town just yesterday, over by the general store."

"And?" Florrie prompted as Alice puffed up in importance.

"Trudy was dressed like a pauper and looked just terrible. I almost went to her, to tell her that I was sorry about Thomas' death, but then her mother walked in."

"What happened next, Alice? Don't be leaving us in suspense," Clara Beth Downy begged, she was on the edge of her seat with anticipation. The end of her graying braid was currently being twisted nervously between two fingers as she listened raptly.

"Her mother pretended that Trudy didn't even exist. The girl tried to greet her, but the woman refused to acknowledge her, even the slightest," Alice recounted. "After she left, Edna Bixby told me in a teary confession mind you, that she was pure positive Trudy had been born with an evil bone."

"*An evil bone*?" the other women echoed in unison.

"Edna claimed that Trudy was glad that her pa was dead and wanted some of the Bixby money for herself. She seemed to think that her daughter had something to do with that useless Vernon boy robbing the bank," Alice imparted. "We all know that when his body was found, there was no money left. Maybe she killed him and stashed the money somewhere?"

"*A set up*!" Florrie gasped.

"That is nonsense Alice," Winnie huffed. "No one is born with evil bones, and if the girl wanted to see her pa dead, she could have done it years ago. As rotten as that Thomas Bixby was, I was surprised no one took it in their mind to help him meet his maker before now."

"Winnie," Melody chided, "That's not nice."

"May not be nice, but it sure is the truth," Winnie confirmed with a nod.

"Poor Mathias," Clara Beth lamented. "He is stuck defenseless in a house with that girl. What if she tries to do away with him? She could be doing all sorts of things to his helpless body!" Clara Beth finished with a dramatic wail.

Clara's plump body draped across her chair indicating, that she was headed toward a proper faint. Fanning herself weakly, Clara, thankfully recovered as she noticed the last sweet biscuit was left on the serving plate. Not one to miss out on an opportunity, Clara sat up and reached for the treat, before slumping back down into her dramatics.

"With a boy that fine, I could tell you what I would be doing," Winnie remarked with a smirk as she made a grab for the baby. Tucking the little one in her arms, the widow cooed down at the babe. "That's for sure little lady, Miss Winnie knows what to do with a handsome fella."

"Like you do with Fergus O'Malley?" Florrie quipped to Winnie's embarrassment, sending the rest of the ladies into fits of uproarious laughter. The sound woke the baby, who let out a howl of protest at having her slumber disturbed.

"Hey now," an old man called out as he shuffled slowly into the room. "What is all this cacklin' about and why is me' lassie crying?"

Fergus O'Malley, otherwise known as "Pops," approached the white haired woman cradling his precious great granddaughter Moira, in her arms. Her white hair and smooth, barely lined skin made only more youthful in appearance as she held the tiny new life, trying to shush her cries.

He didn't know the reason, but of late, Winnie Lawrence danced about his mind more often than not. At first it had annoyed him. Gradually it had intrigued him, but now it had moved to a constant desire to discover just what it was that held him enthralled by the woman.

"Howdy dragon lady," he greeted with a sly whisper as he leaned over to place one aged hand on the infant's back. "Are you here to finally repay your bet?" Bright blue eyes twinkled with devilish delight as he teased her.

"Hush up you fool," Winnie ordered in a hushed tone of her own. "You swore you weren't going to bring that up again," she whispered hotly, her cheeks heating.

"I didn't swear anything of the sort. You owe me that kiss fair and square, but are too yellow to pay up," Fergus denied quietly before once again standing tall. Well, about as tall as his half past five foot height could bring him. "So, what may I ask are you ladies gossiping about today?"

"They are talking about Mathias," Melody tattled. "Miss Florrie here seems to think it is unseemly for Miss Bixby to be staying over at the Bar S without a proper chaperone."

"Is that so?"

Fergus turned his bright blue gaze toward the Pritchard woman. The female was a right harridan, whose own husband hid from her on a daily basis down at the saloon. Fergus had never much cared for the lady, but he did enjoy winning money off of her husband. Good ol' Harold was a lousy poker player, and Fergus didn't want to lose his golden goose by upsetting the Missus.

"Yes Mr. O'Malley," Florrie answered as she preened. "It may truly be all and well, but it doesn't appear that way. Innocent she may be, but others… mean spirited gossips mind you, will just rip that girl's reputation to shreds."

Mean spirited gossips like herself, Fergus thought with contempt. He never could understand those that believed their opinions were superior. He detested harpies that took delight in running down decent folks and putting a bad spin on good deeds. Florrie was one of those hateful women that saw flaws in everyone but her own aging reflection.

"Maybe I should take a jaunt over to Mathias' spread tomorrow and have a word with him?" Fergus suggested to the flapping crow.

He had no real intention of doing so, but he wanted to stop the chinwag in her tracks, before she, herself, headed over there to do the same. Mathias Sinclair was a good and respectful boy, but even he could only be pushed so far. Fergus would wager the skinny witch would be thrown out on her rear end in less time than it took to say 'how ya do.'

Only trouble could come from Mrs. Pritchard's busybody activities, and although Fergus held contempt for the Bixby girl's father, he did not think it right that she be condemned for trying to do a good deed. The girl didn't deserve the town's scorn.

"What a good notion Mr. O'Malley! Having a distinguished gentleman of some years advising Mathias could only be a blessing. An unmarried female should not be residing in the home of a bachelor," Florrie Pritchard said with a nod. "As it is, the girl can no longer hold her head up in society."

"It's true," Clara agreed. "There's been a lot of talk."

"She'll never find a husband now," Florrie announced. "Her poor mother! First her husband is killed and now her daughter disgraces her."

"Well, what if he were to marry her? Would that save her reputation?" Fergus asked thoughtfully.

"It would be a good start," Florrie declared.

"Maybe I'll suggest the possibility to him," Fergus offered.

"Lot of good that will do," Winnie barked out with a laugh. "We all know Mathias Sinclair, and you aren't going to ever going to get him to agree to your scheme. He is too smart for you, old man."

"Want to wager on it Miss Winnie?" Fergus asked slyly. A grin stretched from ear to ear. "Same side wager as the last?" he asked wickedly.

"Double or nothing says that Mathias won't even hear you out," Winnie agreed smugly.

"This time woman, you better pay up," Fergus warned with a sly wink. "St. Valentine's Day is less than a week away, you'd better be prepared to pucker up my friend," Fergus whispered near her ear as he placed a gentle kiss upon the infant's head.

"A week? You think you can do this in less than a week?" Winnie scoffed.

"On me sainted Irish heart, I know I can," Fergus pledged and chose to ignore the snort that followed his declaration.

"If you lose, which you will, what do I get?" Winnie asked.

"A bottle of me' best whiskey should do," the old man offered. "But I won't be losing."

"Save it. You're going to need it to drown your sorrows when you lose. I will take a bushel of your first crop of vegetables come summer."

"Ah lassie, don't be underestimating a man with a burnin' need. I would be mor'n happy to gift you with somethin' other than just me' finest carrots," he said in a husky murmur.

"*Fergus!*" Winnie hissed. She was no innocent Miss, she knew full and well what the rogue was suggesting. The dirty scoundrel!

"You can't back out now, it's a bet," he stated firmly as he turned on his heel and adjusted his cane in his grip.

As a plan formed in his mind, Fergus shot out a hasty farewell to the clucking hens that gathered around the furiously blushing Winnie Lawrence. The women all but ignored him in their desire to know just what in the world their side bet was all about, and how they could wager as well. Fergus smothered a chuckle as he heard Winnie sputter out a weak fib about needing a bushel of carrots as he headed toward the door.

Oh, she needed something from him alright…

He knew there was no way that Winnie would ever admit to the others that she had an interest in Fergus O'Malley… especially since she hadn't yet admitted the truth to the man himself. But the interest was there, he'd bet his best bottle of whiskey on it. Fergus was a patient man, she'd get tired of holding out soon enough, then and only then, he'd make his move.

He quickly shuffled out of the room, now that he had a purpose in mind. Convincing Mathias Sinclair to take a bride was going to be tough going. The boy had hardened his heart long ago against the idea of marriage, and it was going to take some fancy footwork to dance around the stone that was in place. Fergus was determined though; he didn't care what it took. He was going to get that kiss from Winnie Lawrence if it killed him… and Fergus was pretty sure, that by the time he got through with him, Mathias Sinclair was going to darn near attempt to do just that.

As he walked from the house, the cold wind picked up blowing fiercely through the tree line. A storm was brewing, but Fergus was undaunted.

It was too late to set out for the Bar S ranch, so he decided to go find his grandson and fill him in on his newest scheme. He could sure use the boy's help. Now that Gabriel was a happily married man, he should want the same for his friend. Also, if he had any O'Malley blood in those veins of his, Gabriel would jump on the chance for a little excitement. Fergus had raised the boy right, so he knew Gabriel wouldn't deny his request for assistance.

**

"Hell no, Pops." With a firm shake of his head the tall man backed up and held his hands out trying to ward off the trouble concocting in his very own barn.

"Gabe," Fergus said with a sad sigh. "I need your help in convincing Mathias. You know how stubborn he can be when it comes to trusting women."

"You're going to have to do that without me," Gabriel O'Malley stated determinedly. "I've been on the receiving end of your schemes Pops, and there's no way I'm going help while you try to hog tie the man I call friend into marriage."

"I'm not trying to hogtie the man, merely make him see reason."

"What do you have riding on this Pops?" Gabe asked trying to get to the heart of the matter. With Pops there was always a motive.

"I don't know what you mean?" Pops countered, but Gabriel wasn't fooled. That innocent look the old man was giving him was filled with mischief. Something was up.

"You know," Pops pondered aloud, "without my schemes as you call them, you'd never have ended up with Melody."

"Pops, that was different."

"And," the conniving man continued as if Gabriel hadn't spoken. "Without Melody, you'd never have sweet little Moira Elizabeth. Can you imagine never holding her tiny body in your hands?" Fergus held his hands out as if cradling the air for effect. "Or Lily, you know how you dote on the girl. Without a bit of trickery, you'd never have the family you claim now."

"Don't go trying to guilt me into helping you."

Gabriel wasn't going to fall for his tricks, no way, no how.

"How's this then," Fergus snapped obviously upset that his ploy was failing. "If you help me with this one thing, I promise not to cook up anymore stratagems with the council boys for one whole year."

"A whole year, without having to fix your messes?" Gabriel repeated the pledge with a snort. "I don't believe it, how will you keep yourself occupied?"

"Oh, I'll stay busy Gabriel, ye' have me word," Fergus promised, his brogue growing thicker by the minute. "I have a passel of carrots to plant and it's gonna take up all me time, no doubt about that."

Gabriel pondered the sudden gleam in his grandfather's eye for a moment. Strange, he had the feeling that Fergus was actually telling the truth. One whole year of not having to clean up the council boys' madcap plots did sound tempting. He could concentrate his time on Melody and the children without having to worry if Pops set the town on fire again.

"When do we go?" Gabriel finally agreed with a grunt.

"Tomorrow!" Fergus cried out happily. "No time to wait."

"Why the hurry?" Gabe asked suspiciously.

"Springs coming son, no time like the present to lay seed."

As Fergus, happy with his enlistment of force headed to the house, Gabriel watched him go with a grin. The old man would never change, and lord knew Gabe would never want him to. The odd thing was he'd never seen Pops so excited about tending his garden, he'd hoped it wasn't a sign of him slowing down.

As thunder rumbled overhead, Gabriel hoped the sound wasn't a warning of things to come.

***

The thunder and lightning clashing outside had nothing on the storm raging inside the darkened room where Mathias lay. Clenching his teeth against the pain, he concentrated once again, praying for movement. No matter how hard he willed his legs to move, they still remained immobile, discouraging him.

"Goddamn," he groaned in frustration.

After running his *nursemaid* off for the night, Mathias sat alone in his room and cursed his useless legs. The pain in his lower back was persistent as always. If he'd had the strength to curl himself into a ball he would have.

He was tired of the constant agony, and wished that he would've just died that day instead of ending up half the man that he once was. It would have been a merciful blessing.

What kind of a God rewarded a man like this?

Mathias had sworn that he could still feel sensations in his legs, but the doctors had assured him that it would pass in time. They explained the phantom limb phenomenon to him. It seemed that men who'd lost a limb in the war would sometimes swear that they still felt an itch or reflex. Even when the limb had been severed from the body, the mind could still recall it. The doctors weren't quite sure when his feeling would fade, but they promised him it would be soon. Mathias didn't know if he should be relieved or frightened for when that day came.

His mother had stood by his bed weeping into her hands as he'd fought the truth, as he'd begged for the doctor's to end his suffering. Instead, they'd assured him that time would heal his broken soul, just not his body. Doc Bixby had even asked his mother to summon the preacher in hopes that he could counsel his patient, but Mathias had refused. "He didn't want *God*, he wanted his legs to work damned it all," he'd cried out angrily.

Mathias couldn't stand the pitying looks on their faces any longer, so he'd told them to leave and to never return. He couldn't stand the feeling of helplessness.

The only person, who hadn't looked at him as if he were a pitiable creature that day, had been the furious Miss Bixby. She'd actually shouted at him for undoing all of their hard work and for scaring the daylights out of his mother. Hands on hips, the brash woman had given him her opinion on his obstinacy. It was not a nice opinion either. He should've kept the doctors and tossed her from the house. But no, despite his first inclination, Mathias had chosen to ignore her presence all the way up to the gates of his ranch.

For when Mathias had declared he was going home to die, Trudy Bixby had declared she was going there with him. Of course, she stubbornly insisted he wasn't going to croak, and come hail or high-water; she was going along to make sure he didn't make a liar out of her.

Her brother had tried to stop her, Mathias remembered that they'd argued to the point of Sebastian trying to physically drag Trudy home with him, but she'd stayed firm. Slapping her brother's hands from her person, Trudy had announced that she no longer had a home and that if Sebastian wanted to see her, he could come calling at the Bar S.

He had to give it to the girl, she sure was tenacious. For the last month or so, Mathias had given it his all to break her, but she kept coming back for more. He hadn't expected her to stay as long as she had, and had no clue what it was going to take to make her give up as nothing seemed to work. Mathias figured there must be something cracked in that pretty little head of hers, to make her want to stay, and damned if he didn't respect her kind of crazy.

-The heart can only grow on daydreams and wishes-

CHAPTER FIVE

In the back of Etta's sister's wardrobe in a weathered box, the dress had sat discarded. Unwanted that is, until Etta had come across the garment while searching for scraps of material for a quilt she was currently working on. An idea had blossomed in Etta's heart, and before she could stop herself, she'd donned the dress.

It was a bit outdated and the fit was a tad snug across her bosom, but the pale rose material was the softest Etta Howard had ever felt. Surprisingly, the color seemed to suit her as well. If she removed a few of the flounces and girlish bows, it would be perfect for Etta to wear for her first dinner out with Tex Brody.

She still could not believe that she had gotten up the nerve to bid on his courtship. He was so strong and masculine, that very fact should have had her running for cover... but she felt odd little flutters in her stomach whenever he smiled his crooked smile at her. She knew that he would not be considered handsome at least not in the general sense. Tex was too rugged, rough, and scarred, but he was magnificent to her.

Etta was concerned that he would not be receptive to her, as she was a plain spinster woman with nothing to recommend her but a pair of child bearing hips and a stack of well-worn books. She also had an overbearing mother that came with the deal, but Etta was determined to try to make her dreams come true.

Sighing Etta shook those thoughts away. She would concentrate on the positives... One: Tex had smiled and inclined his head to her instead of running for the hills, when he'd learned of her signing his bachelor ledger. Two: she had just purchased a copy of the guide to running the perfect household, by Rupert Maxwell. With such wise tidbits of insight, how could she fail?

The dress was a few inches too long in the hem and needed to be let out a couple inches about her waist and bust line, but she reckoned it would not be too hard of a task to accomplish before her big night.

Twirling about, Etta almost danced with joy. She knew that she was considered plain and mousy, but standing in this dress, she could almost believe she was somewhat fetching. That was something she longed to be. If only for one night… for only one man, Etta wanted to be something close to pretty.

At twenty six years old, she knew that it was a slim chance that Tex would pick her over the younger, prettier girls, but Etta had only one man in mind as she had waited for the crowd to thin around the bachelor ledgers on the night of the bid. She had pinned her hopes with her last three pennies onto him.

There was something about Mr. Brody that drew Etta to him. Sadness about his eyes that Etta knew no one else had bothered to notice. Most people could not see past his massive size and prison record, but Etta could.

Tex had always been polite to her the few times she had come in close proximity to him. Countless times she had gawked embarrassingly at him through the window of his store front, watching as he worked. She had marveled at his creations and wished she had just enough pin money to purchase just one of his beautiful carved candles. If only to own something that he had created.

Unfortunately for Etta, Mama had cut her allowance by half because Daisy Lynn had written and announced she and her husband had fallen on hard times. If Mama could just send them a bit to tide them over for a few months, Daisy would be ever so appreciative, as it was hard to entertain the society matrons of Boston without available funds. The Howard family themselves had fallen on hard times after Etta's daddy had passed, but if Daisy wanted something, then their mama made sure she got it.

"Get out of that dress right now missy! That's Daisy Lynn's," at the furious cry from the open doorway, Etta froze instantaneously. Her mama was up from her afternoon nap and in one of her moods.

"Daisy left it here Mama," Etta reminded her mother. "I just thought that maybe if I altered it, I could use it myself. I promise not to ruin the material," she explained.

"Daisy will be back someday soon Etta, I know that for a fact, and you will not steal from her do you understand me?"

Walking over to where her daughter stood, Vera Howard grabbed Etta roughly by her arm and forced her to face the gilded vanity mirror that Daisy had once been so proud of. The mirror, like everything else in her life, she had left without once glance behind.

"Look at yourself Etta. You are like an owl trying to pass yourself off as a dove." Vera clucked, "Do you honestly want to embarrass yourself dressed like this? Do you want to embarrass me?"

"No mama," Etta whispered instantly ashamed. The last thing she wanted to do was make herself appear like any more of a fool.

Tugging at the bodice of the dress Vera announced, "You are far plumper than Daisy ever was, you can't possibly wear this... you'll tear the seams out."

"Yes Mama,' Etta hung her head and hid the tears that formed in her eyes.

"Heavens be, I don't know what has gotten into you girl. Ever since that bank robbery last month, you haven't been the same," Vera complained. "If I don't reign in on you more, I'm afraid that you'll turn out like that trollop Bixby girl."

"Mama, Trudy saved me in that robbery. I think—"

"You think what Etta?" Vera snapped interrupting Etta from defending the other woman. "That girl has gone and ruined her family's good name. Her poor mother! Why, I would just die if she were my daughter!"

"I know Mama, but—"

Trudy stopped herself from explaining what occurred in the bank that day, and how Trudy had selflessly offered herself to the villain. Etta knew that Trudy had only done it so that she could distract him enough to allow the women to escape his clutches. It was the bravest thing that Etta had ever seen in all her born days, and she wished that she could be more like Trudy.

"I don't know where you're thinking you'll be going dressed so fancified anyway. I told that Tex Brody that I wouldn't be allowing him to court you. Don't you go thinking that I will be changing my mind on the subject," Vera huffed.

"I know you don't want me to see him but—"

"Not another word Etta! Now, get out of that dress and get started on the mending, we haven't got all day to lollygag about," Vera warned sternly before charging out of the room.

The door slamming in her wake sent a wave of sickness through Etta. When her mama was unhappy, Etta's life was made miserable. Vera Howard's constant complaints would only worsen, her tantrums would become uncontrollable.

"Yes ma'am," Etta spoke to an empty room. She walked over and slumped herself onto the bed and sighed sadly.

Why couldn't mama see that her beloved daughter hadn't been home since the day she had run off five years ago? Daisy had always been looking for a fancier lifestyle for herself. Even her handsome fiancée, Mathias Sinclair, had not been good enough for her. It didn't matter to Daisy, that with a toss of her midnight curls, she had fled the territory and broken his heart.

Etta loved her sister, but she knew her faults. Daisy was spoiled, conceited, and self-absorbed just to name a few. Vera had taken to her bed in misery bemoaning the loss of her wayward daughter for months, while her husband Hiram, had sat silently; a sad smile graced his face. Etta knew that her papa had been aware of the fact that Daisy Lynn had been embarrassed by living as a simple farmer's daughter.

Hiram Howard had been a proud man who owned a small plot of land and grew vegetables and raised chickens to sell in town. He was a quiet soul who preferred reading rather than socializing, much to his wife's disgust. In many ways, Etta was like her papa, a fact that she rather relished. She missed her father every day and had cried rivers of tears when he had collapsed one spring day in his garden that he had loved so much. Hiram Sinclair had gone to his reward that very night, and left Etta alone to face Vera and her constant demands.

Mama had tried to get them to hold papa's funeral in order for Daisy to attend, but they had no time to wait. It was fortunate that they had not, for Daisy sent a telegraph informing their mama that she would not be attending Papa's service, but she expected the plain gold band Papa had worn as his wedding ring. Daisy claimed that as the only married daughter she, Daisy, should be allowed to give the ring to her new husband Percy Pylright. This was a shock to the family, not that Daisy had demanded her portion of papa's worldly goods... no, the shock was that Daisy had been married for some time to a man no one had heard of. She hadn't even offered the courtesy of informing her fiancée here in town that the wedding they had planned together could no longer take place. That chore had fallen on Etta. It had been one of the hardest things that she'd been forced to do.

Poor Mathias Sinclair had believed that once Daisy had gotten city life out of her system, she would return and settle down as his bride, but he'd been wrong. Mathias had sat stonily as Etta had stuttered out every damning word. He hadn't even uttered a sound as she had informed him that Daisy had taken a new last name, but Etta knew he was broken inside. Mathias had quietly thanked Etta, walked her to her buggy and told her to tell Daisy – if she ever wrote her, that he wished Daisy achieved everything she dreamed of.

Her sister had never deserved Mathias Sinclair, Etta thought sadly.

After it became clear that Etta and her mother couldn't work the farm without her father, they had sold out and moved into a small house behind the livery that Etta's great uncle Baxter had graciously gifted to them. In order to support the two of them, Etta took in mending and helped out at her great uncle's livery. She really didn't mind working with Uncle Baxter, he was patient and praised her regularly. The added delight of working with the horses kept there was a blessing on most days. Etta, short on friends, sometimes spoke her every thought to the animals. They never laughed at her. In fact, they were always glad to see her coming. Etta knew it was more for the oats she carried in her pail, but she pretended they thought of her as a friend as well.

Rising from the bed, Etta redressed in her faded, gray work dress and placed the beautiful gown once again back where she'd found it.

Stiffening her spine, Etta resolved to find a way to capture the heart of the man she fancied. She may not be able to do it through her looks, or her cooking skills that were also sadly lacking, but she would think of something. She had to. The future that she faced was too bleak to contemplate. For if Etta didn't marry, she would be stuck tied to her mother's apron strings for the rest of her natural born life, and that was a terrible prospect to face.

Etta wanted to be a bride, but she desired nothing as much as the thought of becoming Tex Brody's bride. She'd just have to do it without the beautiful dress that she had hoped to wear.

As Etta grabbed her mending and got to work, she couldn't help but daydream of the life that she'd longed for. It was the one thing her mother couldn't take from her. At least in her mind, Etta could live as exciting a life as Trudy Bixby did. She could wear the prettiest of gowns and flirt with the man that she yearned for and no one was ever the wiser. No one could mock her for it. Dreams were the only place she was safe from scorn.

***

The moon would be full and high in starlit sky. Her dress, delicate and flowing in the most gossamer of silk, would be the lightest of pink... no, no, a bold, peacock blue, cut daringly low. The lace trim would swish about her ankles as her handsome partner twirled her about to the slow, soft strains of violins. On through the night they would dance as if she were lighter than air. He'd glance down at her laughing face and their eyes would meet. Suddenly, he would pull her closer; a look would appear in his eyes. Her breath would hitch as he leaned in ever so closer, his mouth nearly pressed to hers. Finally, just when she felt that her heart would burst from her chest if he didn't kiss her that moment, he lowered his mouth over hers and—

"Miss Trudy, are you listening?"

"Hmmm?" Trudy glanced up and sighed as her daydream was interrupted just as it was getting good, by a smiling Annie Culver.

The woman who acted as housekeeper on the Bar S was at current thumping a heavy wooden paddle against a badly beaten metal tub in continuous whacks. A second tub filled high with steaming water sat beside, awaiting use. The basket piled tall with linens that sat nearby, brought a grimace to Trudy's face as she realized just what sort of work was in store for her today.

"Maybe I shouldn't be leaving you with the laundry chore so soon. The look in your eye tells me that you're already regretting your offer to help me today," Annie alleged with a chuckle.

"I want to help, I really do," Trudy promised.

It was the truth, she did want to help. Trudy genuinely liked Annie Culver. The woman happened to be painfully shy, but once out of her shell was quite the pistol. Annie was about the only one on the ranch that even spoke a kind word to her. The quiet woman had gone out of her way to make Trudy feel welcome instead of the interloper that she truly was. And for that, Trudy would be forever grateful to Annie. A few chores would never be repayment enough.

"Maybe instead, you'd rather be twirling across that dance floor you've been muttering about," Annie asked slyly and Trudy blushed to the roots of her hair.

"Ah," Annie tsked when Trudy began to stammer an apology. "Don't be sorry, I myself used to daydream as a girl," she confided. "Oh, to be young again!"

"You are far from your dotage," Trudy scoffed.

The housekeeper was older than Trudy by a good ten years, though she still radiated a youthful appearance. Her long, raven hued braids were perfectly plaited. They gleamed in the sunshine drawing Trudy's envy, as her own hair was knotted up into a clumsy attempt at a chignon. Trudy was still not used to arranging her own hair and missed her maid, Maud, from the depth of her rotten soul. The poor dear was left to her mother's largess now that Trudy was banned from the house, so it was a good possibility that Maud was missing Trudy just as much right about now.

"Sorry Annie," Trudy confessed, "my mind wandered for a second time. Could you explain the process again to me?"

"Once the clothing has been scrubbed on the washboard, we use this paddle to them move them to the second tub. Like so," Annie explained while demonstrating her superb wash day routine. It was a routine that Trudy had never in her life dreamed she'd ever take part in, nor would it have been a fond wish to observe, but Annie needed her help and Trudy was determined to assist to the best of her limited abilities.

Besides, helping with laundry day got Trudy time away from the dreaded grump of a man that brooded above stairs. A man that resembled a little too much like Trudy's recently imagined suitor, for her peace of mind. Though her dream man looked a lot like Mathias Sinclair one thing separated them in her mind. Her imaginary fellow was nice to her.

A shiver ran up her spine as she thought about Mathias. The man had been extra surly with her this morning after the latest incident. She hadn't meant to drop his coffee onto him, but the tray had been overly heavy this morning, and she'd been in such a hurry. He hadn't needed to make such a fuss about it in her opinion. By the way Mathias had howled you'd think the front of his night shirt was on fire instead of merely splashed with his morning drink. And, Trudy had offered to help him remove the drenched cloth and change into another shirt. It wasn't her fault that when she'd tried to inspect the reddened skin of his chest he'd nearly choked on the sweet biscuit that Annie had baked to go along with his coffee. She'd always heard butter was good for soothing burns, and had idea why he'd been so adverse to her idea of rubbing him down with it. But for some reason he'd objected and ordered her from his room.

"Make sure that you secure the clothes properly with the pins, else they'll fall from the clothesline and need to be rewashed," Annie warned, drawing Trudy's attention back to the chore at hand.

"I will," Trudy promised. She had no plans to rewash anything, once would be plenty enough for her.

As Annie headed into the house to peel a mountain of potatoes for her promised soup, Trudy set to work.

It only took thirty minutes of scrubbing, before Trudy developed a strong respect for the maids that her father had employed. Within an hour's work, she had a pile of freshly scrubbed clothes awaiting the wringer and was quite proud of herself. The work was hard and her hands were cramping painfully as she scrubbed the dickens out of the only other pair of drawers that she owned, but it felt rewarding.

Just as she'd squeezed as much excess water as she could from her unmentionables and began to hang them on the line, a lapping sound came from behind. Spinning Trudy's jaw dropped. The biggest, ugliest, dog in all the territory sat drinking from her clean water tub. His great jowls dripping his salivation into the now cooled water. The dirt on his brown coat muddying the remaining clothes in the tub, and Trudy saw red. She'd just spent all of that time scrubbing those garments!

"Shoo!" Trudy hissed in anger.

The dog enjoying his refreshment chose to ignore her. His big paws reached into the tub nearly tipping it. He batted playfully at the water as if in search for something.

"Go on now!" Trudy ordered once again, this time with more authority. There was no way she was going to let the beast drink up all her hard work.

Walking toward the mongrel she flapped her hands wildly hoping to scare him off. Instead, the drawers she held in her hand seemed to intrigue the horrible demon. With a happy woof, he charged. Leaping at Trudy's hands, the dog attacked the cloth.

"Give me those drawers you fiend!" Trudy cried as she clung to the other end of the material.

The dog, taking her resistance as a game, tossed his wide head wildly and growled low in his throat. Planting his large paws deeper into the dirt, the animal moved slowly backward dragging Trudy along with him. There was a shredding sound as one leg of the garment began to tear away from the seat.

Eyes wide, Trudy squealed "Annie!" at the top of her lungs. She had no plans on becoming the monster's meal. She would not die her ripped drawers in hand!

"Annie, grab your gun!" she shouted toward the house.

"Damn mutt," she heard mumbled as an irate man waltzed up to the dog and grabbed his massive neck by the scruff.

"Mr. Culver, please be careful," Trudy begged. Though she did not know the man well, she had no wish to see her new friend widowed over a piece of ladies' undergarments.

"Drop it!" Patrick Culver ordered the pilfering canine.

The dog, sensing his playtime over, dropped the now filthy garment at his feet and sat back on his haunches. Trudy blinked as she watched the dog's face transform into something close to a grin as he panted roughly.

"That thing is smiling at me!" Trudy announced to Mr. Culver as if he didn't have eyes for himself.

"Trudy!" Annie shouted as she came, gun toting, onto the scene. "What's happened?" Annie asked her husband as Trudy continued to stare in disbelief at the grinning hound.

"Miss Bixby here has just met up with the O'Malley's dog."

"Oh dear," Annie sighed. "I forgot to warn you that Mr. Crinkles likes to visit on wash day. It's almost as if the sweet boy can smell the lye a mile away," she informed Trudy as she reached over and scratched the mutt under his chin.

"Lye?" Trudy mumbled as the dog's ears perked up in his wrinkled head.

"He has a partiality for it. I try to get the clothes hung right away, or he'll take off with them. He has a strange fondness for dragging freshly washed linens through the dirt. It's a game to him."

"Well," Trudy huffed as she surveyed the damage, "he certainly won this round."

"I'll be back to empty the wash tubs when you're through playing out here," Culver announced curtly before turning on heel. "Come on Mr. Crinkles, Beaux will want to see you."

Trudy watched as the dog trotted alongside the ranch foreman as if he hadn't a care in the world. Of course he truly didn't, it wasn't he that would be rewashing the laundry.

As Annie instructed her on how to pump fresh water into the now empty tub, Trudy was glad that at least her day couldn't get any worse.

***

She'd only meant to clean the chimney, not become part of it.

Two thoughts swirled about Trudy's mind as she stood stalk still in the constricted space. One, she was horribly ignorant for tempting fate and two, for once in her life she was thankful that the good lord hadn't blessed her with an overly large, cumbersome bosom, else she'd have absolutely no way out of the blasted mess that she currently found herself in.

The space was too tight for her to bend her knees and wiggle downward, but she tried to anyway, hoping that she was wrong. She wasn't. Trudy was definitely stuck and didn't want the man in the bed to know it.

"I think you've been in there long enough," Mathias called out smugly and Trudy groaned.

He was on to her predicament and she knew it.

"Tru—"

"Shut up! Just shut your trap right this second!" She snapped in return as she tried without success to breathe in the dark soot that coated the brick walls.

"I know you're stuck in there," Mathias called out. "Just say the word and I'll shout for Annie."

"Annie brought the men their noon meal, so she won't hear you," Trudy informed him sourly with a stomp of her foot.

Her arms were getting tired as they'd been raised above her head for so long, and her rear end was starting to ache something fierce from her cramped position.

"Math—" she tried to call out but ended up only coughing as she inhaled too much ash.

Trudy was starting to become alarmed. As her fear rose, her breathing became labored and she sobbed unable to catch a lungful of air. She didn't want to die in this blasted tomb of a chimney with that man looking on.

"Try to slide yourself out," Mathias encouraged her; all humor quickly vanishing from his tone as he heard her broken cry.

"I'm trying to!" she wailed as she wiggled like a trout on a fisherman's line.

No matter how hard she tried, her hips and derriere prevented her from sliding out. In panic, she tried to climb further into the flue, hoping that gravity would help dispel her, only find herself stuck further.

"Listen to me," Mathias encouraged. "Listen to my voice Honey, just my voice okay?"

"K," she sniffled, hoping to the heavens that he heard her over the beating of her heart which was pounding in her ears that very second. She felt lightheaded and nauseous and only wanted to close her eyes.

"Don't do that!" he ordered making her realize that she said that last thought aloud.

She had a tendency to do that. Talking to herself always calmed her when she was nervous.

"Don't be nervous, we can get you out of there."

Would she ever stop talking aloud?!

"Tru," Mathias spoke louder, trying to gain her attention and make himself heard through the thick wall. "Concentrate on my voice. Breathe shallow breaths, do you understand? Not too deep, just slow your breathing down. I'm going to count to four, each time I reach four, take in some air and release it."

As Mathias counted, Trudy began to focus on the deep timbre of his voice. She breathed in when he ordered her to and released it when he'd commanded her. Slowly, she felt herself relax and the buzzing in her head receded.

"Okay Sugar, now I want you to take one deep breath in, and while you're holding it, slip downward."

It took three tries until her feet finally touched the ledge of the mantle and she nearly passed out in relief.

"That's it, Sweetheart," Mathias encouraged, "just a bit further. You're nearly there."

When her bottom finally cleared the flue and descended into the opening of the fireplace, Mathias sighed in relief, his heart slowed in pace. As she plopped out of the small brick structure, he wished he could go to her, snatch her up and give her the shaking of a lifetime.

Jesus! What had he been thinking to order her to clean his fireplace? He'd only thought to give her the dirtiest job in the room to do. Next to emptying his chamber pot, which she'd already done, he'd thought that she balk at getting filthy and leave him be. He'd never expect the daft woman to climb all the way into the shaft and get herself stuck.

His chest ached as he thought about what could have happened to her had she suffocated in there, with him watching, useless, unable to come to her aid.

As Trudy stumbled toward the bed, tears streaming down her grimy face, Mathias waited for the slap that never came. Instead of battering him as she ought to do, the peculiar woman threw herself into his arms and wept rivers upon his chest.

Mathias, unsure as to what to do to calm her, ran a hand over her knotted hair and pressed a light kiss to her brow as she curled up beside him on the bed.

"Shh, shh," he whispered. "You're fine now."

For long minutes they lay in silence, until Mathias cleared his throat and asked her if she was fully recovered from her fright.

"I hate the dark," she confessed in a whisper. "But now I think I hate small spaces even more!"

Mathias bit his tongue from telling her that she had nothing to fear as long as he was around. What a fool thing to think, let alone say! He was of no use to her and she needed to realize that now. They both did.

He wanted her gone from his room, away from his life, as soon as possible. Every day that he spent with her only reminded Mathias of everything that he'd lost, and everything that couldn't be between them.

"So," he asked with as much arrogance as he could muster, "do you plan to just laze about all day?"

"I—"

"I'm not in the market for a lap dog," he informed her coldly and tried not to regret his words as she shot from the bed, a frown upon her face.

"You—" she sputtered.

"You might as well go earn your keep by cleaning out the ash barrel, you can't get any filthier," he snickered.

As she left his room in a miserable gloom, Mathias told himself that it was for the best. The woman had no place in his bed or by his side.

-A man's own mind can be his greatest enemy-

CHAPTER SIX

The Bar S was in full stir as the O'Malley buggy pulled up to the main house. With a plan in mind, the men nodded at each other and dismounted.

"Let me do all the talking," Fergus ordered.

"You always do," his grandson replied with a nod.

Fergus chose to ignore the quip. It was near on to supper time, and he'd high hopes that Miss Annie, the housekeeper, would have made enough to spare his poor soul a quick bite.

As he glanced up at the monstrosity that Mathias Sinclair called home, he grimaced. The place was too big and too elaborately detailed in Fergus' estimation. It hardly fit into the tradition of a ranch house. Tall, white columns adorned the front of the structure, as wide windows with whitewashed shutters nearly shouted out the expense it took to build such a dwelling. It was a beautiful home to be sure, but Fergus knew that it had been built for all the wrong reasons. Shaking his head sadly, the old man steeled his resolve about what he'd come here to do.

Limping a bit due to his gout, Fergus made his way up the porch. Knocking on the wide front door, he waited patiently as Gabriel shifted nervously beside him. The boy not used to scheming was going to be a hindrance if he didn't get himself under control.

"Mr. O'Malley, Pops!" a voice greeted as the door swung open moments later revealing a lovely woman in a plain dress. The look on her face suggested to Fergus that there hadn't been many visitors to the Bar S ranch since Mathias' shooting, and now she had two on her hands.

"Miss Trudy," Fergus greeted, doffing his hat. "How're ye faring this fine day?" he asked politely, although he could tell she'd seen better days. Harried, would be the polite term to use for her appearance. Trudy's hair was in disarray and her face smudged with black.

"Please come in," Trudy prompted the men as she stepped away from the entry.

"Miss Trudy," Gabriel nodded politely as he held out his hat in a show of respect.

"I see you've been busy here," Fergus remarked with a glance about the lower level of the house.

"I'm assuming you've come to see Mr. Sinclair," Trudy said with a bright smile. The stark white of her teeth stood out against the grime coating her face, and Fergus winced. The girl was a right mess.

"You have a bit of...?" Fergus informed her with a point to the tip of her nose.

"Oh!" Trudy squeaked as she lifted a hand to wipe at the tiny button that was her nose. Unfortunately her hands were as filthy as her face, so she'd just made the smudging worse.

Fishing into his pocket for a clean square of linen, Fergus handed the woman the handkerchief and watched as the crisp white material turned the shade of coal.

"I'm so sorry," she apologized for the destruction of the cloth. "I was sweeping the chimney in Mathias' room."

"At this time of day?" Fergus asked astounded.

"Mathias is in a mood today. He decided after I brought him his luncheon that he wanted the hearth in his room cleaned thoroughly, so I decided to do oblige him" she explained her filthy state. "I'm just about to go clean the ash barrel."

"Clean the ash barrel?" Gabriel inquired. "Why would you do such a thing?"

"Mathias asked me to."

"Where's Annie?" Fergus asked referring to the shy woman who filled the role as housekeeper on the Bar S. He shot a look to his grandson that said, 'say no more, you fool.'

"She's taking inventory of our food stores before I plan my next trip into town for supplies," Trudy explained.

"Well me' dear, you might as well show us up to the grouser, and then I suggest you go find Annie, and both of you ladies cover your ears... I have a feeling that some choice words will be flying around up here."

"Threaten him with vinegar wash in his mouth if he gets discourteous, that's what I do," Trudy instructed before taking Fergus' arm and escorting him slowly up the wide staircase.

Gabriel followed silently behind, wisely keeping his opinions to himself.

"Vinegar you say?" Fergus asked, one brow rose, "Does it work?"

"Not in the least," she confessed. "He's as sour as ever, but I keep hoping it eventually will."

"You keep tryin' me love," Fergus encouraged. "A good woman never gives up on taming her man." Fergus announced as they came upon the closed door to Mathias' room.

"Mathias Sinclair is not my man, Pops," Trudy explained softly. "I am his nurse that's all."

"Let us see if we can change that, aye?"

As Trudy gaped down at him, Fergus patted Trudy's cheek gently and winked. Removing her hand from his arm, Fergus reached out and turned the knob intending to enter the room.

"Gabe, ye ready me' lad?" he called to his grandson.

"If I wasn't," Gabe uttered, "I don't think that'd stop you."

"Right you'd be," Pops chuckled as he began to enter the room.

"What do you want? It's not supper time," an angry male voice called out before

Fergus could push the door any wider than an arms width. "I've told you to stop hanging 'round my room like a hound without a home." Trudy standing by Fergus' side, stiffened at the insult.

"Oh dear, I see what you mean," Fergus tsked as he once again patted the girl. "Go on and see to getting yourself cleaned up lassie, I'll handle the dragon. I've had some practice in dealing with em' of late."

Without bothering to see if Trudy did as he'd bid, Fergus pushed the door all the way open and stepped inside.

"Do you ever listen to a word I say woman? I told you that I didn't want visitors!" Mathias thundered to the woman who'd obviously chosen to ignore Fergus' offer and instead braved the lion's den.

"Don't go blaming the girl," the old man interjected. "I let me'self in and lucky for you, I brought a gift," Fergus said as he pulled a battered flask from his pocket. "A taste of the brew me and the boys have been working on," he announced as he limped toward the bed.

"Why anyone would want to visit such a growling bear, I will never know!" Trudy remarked under her breath, but Mathias heard her well enough, judging by the scowl he shot her in return.

"Matt," Gabe greeted as he finally decided to enter the sick room. "Had a mind to come on over and see if you were in need of anything."

"A good cup of Arbuckle's would sure come in handy, but don't give it to her to serve, or you'll be wearing it," Mathias spoke with a frown.

"It was an accident!" Trudy cried out in defense.

"You can leave now," Mathias spoke without bothering to look in her direction. His deep voice so filled with disapproval, washed over her and Trudy shuddered.

"I'll be back in an hour." Trudy sniffed as she walked toward the door. She was, as always, offended by his tone. She couldn't understand why Mathias would not let her make her part in his injury up to him. She was trying for heaven's sake!

"Don't bother," he snapped in response as he directed his attention onto her defiant nature. "I don't need you."

"What you need is a bath. As you cannot perform the chore yourself, I guess you're stuck with me," Trudy snapped. "So, stop trying to fight me!"

She turned to him and tried to glare him into backing down, but she should have known better than to attempt it. The action never seemed to benefit her because he did the same to her, and his glare was much more ferocious.

Mathias, reclined in the wide bed, propped against a mountain of pillows. The simple spun cotton nightshirt he wore gaped open at the neck, exposing a bit of light brown chest hair. The tawny locks of his hair were in serious need of a trim, a shadow of a beard forming upon his strong jaw, Mathias' gaze was watchful. He reminded her of a mountain lion ready to pounce, but unable to. A glimmer of frustration shone in his beautiful eyes. The power in his massive frame was sadly restrained by his immobility.

"Don't look so put out sweetheart, we both know that you enjoy the chore," he ground out.

"I beg your pardon?" Trudy retorted. Her nose shot up in the air at the implication.

"Admit it. You get your enjoyment from sneaking peeks of my... manly form." Mathias chuckled dryly and a shiver ran up Trudy's spine.

"I don't know what you're going on about," she denied.

Trudy's cheeks bloomed bright red. The stubborn fool was right. She did like this time of day, and was ashamed to admit it.

Trudy felt flushed at the thought of stripping him bare and caring for him. Her enjoyment of the act was not the thrill of running the cloth over his exposed flesh. It wasn't from watching as the hard planes of his stomach clench at the feel of her hands as they rubbed in the liniment that her brother had provided to prevent bed sores on his muscular body. No, it was the look in his eye that brought her pleasure. It was the only time, that he did not have that look of disdain within the depths of his eyes for her. Something else, something exciting, shone in them and Trudy was drawn to him. She was pulled toward that look, more than she cared to admit. She was a moth to his flame, and hated herself for the weakness.

"It's not as he makes it sound," she protested. She didn't want the other men in the room to think that she was some kind of debauched lookie-lou.

They always kept a large cloth over that certain part of his personal anatomy that a lady was forbidden to see, out of respect to her unmarried state. Not that propriety allowed for her to be bathing an invalid man that was not a relative, but she couldn't give a fig about what was right or proper. Mathias needed her whether he cared to admit it or not. She wasn't going to allow him to humiliate her and make her give up. She was not born addled; Trudy knew that's what he was after.

"Behave yourself sir or I may just have to drown you," Trudy bravely retorted not wanting him to know how deep his barbs struck.

"I'd like to see you try!" he called out from behind her. "Oh, and Trudy?"

"Yes?" she huffed. Turning on heel, she pasted on a false smile.

"The window hangings are getting a bit dusty in here. You'll need to take them down and beat them."

"*I'll beat something by God*," she grumbled irritably.

"What was that?" Mathias asked.

"Nothing."

Fergus took a seat in the empty chair next to the bed and picked up the book that the invalid man had been reading. He leafed through it as he listened to the pair bicker a bit. Mathias, figuring he'd laid down the law, gave more orders for Trudy to complete before the day was out. As the young woman narrowed her eyes and tapped a toe, Fergus knew that Mathias was in for some serious groveling if their plan were to turn out accordingly.

The old man sighed deeply as Trudy stomped out of the room. Oh yes, Fergus had his work cut out for him.

"What brings you both by?" Mathias inquired as a door slammed in the distance.

"We've come about yer' problem son," Fergus stated.

"My problem?" Mathias queried, one brow raised. "What's he talking about?" he asked his friend.

"Matt—" Gabe groaned, obviously buckling under the weight of his conscience.

"Oh, aye... your marriage problem. I have a solution you see," Fergus announced happily, interrupting whatever his grandson would have said. He couldn't afford to let Gabe natter on like a silly tittle-tattle.

"Marriage problem? Fergus, have you tibbled yourself stupid?" Mathias asked. "I told Alec that you boys shouldn't be allowed to concoct your own brew recipes."

"No, I'm sober as a pope, but here," Fergus said holding out the flask, "have a nip."

With a shrug, Mathias took a healthy swallow. The taste wasn't too bad he considered. There was quite a kick to the amber malt that might actually sell well. The crazy old men might actually be on to something!

"I'm impressed," he admitted. "I didn't think you boys could brew something this adequate.

"Oh, bless," Pops waved away the praise sheepishly.

Mathias was going for his second swig, when Fergus announced, "You'll be weddin' Miss Trudy."

Mathias promptly choked on the fiery liquid.

Pops, quicker on his feet than the men had given him credit for, jumped up and pounded him on the back and ordered him to raise his arms so he could beat the air back into him. His grandson seeing Mathias' distress pulled Pops off of him and grabbed the flask before the precious brew could spill upon the bedding.

"Have you lost your mind Pops?" Mathias rasped as he rubbed his raw throat. "Gabe, are you hearing this?"

"I'm thinking that Pops may be right on this one," Gabe admitted.

"Come on boy, hear me out," Fergus pleaded as Mathias stared in horror at his friend. "It's not as though it's a bad idea."

"A bad idea? Hell no Pops. It's a horse shit idea, that's what it is!" Mathias Sinclair roared furiously. "Why in the world would you want me to marry that woman?" he demanded.

"It makes perfect sense to me. Trudy Bixby needs a home, and you're in need of a bride," Fergus stated as he drummed his fingers on his thigh. He knew Mathias would react badly to his plan, but Fergus had come armed to the fight. He would wait and give the boy a chance to change his mind, before he used his argument against him.

"It's best to nip all talk of impropriety in the bud," Fergus announced firmly.

"What impropriety?" Mathias wanted to know.

"Her staying here hasn't been looked at too kindly," Gabe informed him when Fergus just gave Mathias a knowing look.

"I'm in no need of a bride, and if I were, Trudy Bixby would be the last one that I'd choose."

"Why's that?" Fergus asked. "She seems a nice sort."

"I can't marry her," Mathias said flatly, ignoring Fergus' questioning.

"Why not?" Fergus demanded once again.

"Because I… I just can't, and that is the end of it."

"If I have to, I will go straight on over to your mama's and put a bug into her ear about what's being said about the girl," Fergus warned. "Charlotte may be busy caring for George about now, but she won't be too happy to know that her son is refusin' to do the right thing by the girl. I suspect she'll descend on you like the wrath of Jehovah."

"Pops," Mathias growled in warning.

"Don't you 'Pops' me," Fergus thundered. "I've known you a long time boy, and never in my life have I been ashamed to call you friend." Fergus shook his head sadly before continuing on. "Trudy Bixby needs to be protected from those harpies and their gossip. She's a woman without a family now."

"Matt," Gabriel cut in, "the girl has been shunned. With her father dead and her brother refusing to acknowledge her, she has no men folk to protect her. You and I both know what that means for a woman out here."

"I'm not the one who killed her pa!" Mathias roared in response to his friend's logic.

"No, but you are all that she has now," Fergus cut in. "You need to marry the girl... unless you aren't man enough to handle the lass. That can't be it...can it?" Fergus asked slyly. "You're not afraid of the girl are you?"

"That's horse sh—"

"You are!" Fergus cried out, "You're afraid of her alright."

"Fergus," Mathias growled, "listen here—"

"No, you listen here," Fergus snapped, "there are a lot of men talking about making Miss Trudy an indecent proposition." Fergus shook his head sadly and tut- tutted a bit. "Talk is that she's been playing loose for you, so she may as well do for them too."

"What men?" Mathias thundered. "Gabe, is this true?"

"Yes," Gabe admitted, "there's been some crude talk around the Rot Gut."

"Don't disappoint me son," Fergus stated as he opened the door. "If you don't help the girl, then you're not half the man I thought you were," the old man remarked as he walked out of the room.

Heading out the way he came, Gabe stopped at the door and regarded his sullen friend. "This is Serena all over again, but this time it's you, not Alec, dishonoring a woman," he announced.

"It's not the same at all. I haven't touched Trudy Bixby," Mathias denied.

"I see the way you look at her Matt; and if that little spat is any indication, it's only a matter of time until you do," Gabe chuckled wryly. "And, judging by the soot that you're wearing, you haven't exactly kept her at arm's length either.

When Mathias gaze shot down to examine his filthy night shirt, he let out a foul curse. A small black handprint rested against his heart, making a liar out of him.

"I've been where you are, and if you're wondering, the parson's trap isn't so bad," Gabriel assured him knowingly.

Mathias said nothing in return. He'd never thought he'd see the day that Gabe O'Malley would turn moon eyed and follow in his matchmaking grandfather's shoes.

"Besides, you know Pops won't quit until you see things his way."

"No I won't!" the old man cried out from beyond the door, obviously eavesdropping on their conversation.

As Gabe shook his head ruefully and marched from the room, Mathias mulled over Fergus' words. "Not half the man I thought you were."

"Yeah, Pops," Mathias whispered to the closed door as pain once again lanced through his back, "but the problem is, I'm no longer a man at all."

No matter how tempting the notion was, no matter how good she felt to hold in his arms, he couldn't force a girl like her into accepting only half a man. Women always wanted something better, and he could never be that.

***

The men found Trudy in the kitchen drowning her sorrows in Annie's cider and large hunks of cornbread. She'd washed up as best she could and changed into her only other clean dress, but no matter how hard she tried, she couldn't wash the memory of being stuck in that chimney from her mind.

"There ye are lass!" Fergus crowed as he limped into the room and took a seat. "Don't you worry none," he announced with a grin, "we set the boy to rights."

Trudy, mouth full, decided to let that pass. She honestly didn't want to know what he was nattering on about.

Annie, busy at the stove, grabbed up two bowls and ladled out a healthy portion of soup. Without having to ask, Annie placed the bowls before the men and smiled as they each complimented both her mind reading ability and her cooking skills.

"I noticed the ambulatory chair in the front parlor," Gabe began as he pinched a piece of cornbread for himself. "Wouldn't it be better served in his room?"

"He won't use it," Trudy answered offhandedly as she buttered another slice and handed it to Fergus.

"Why's that?"

"He thinks it'll be too hard to get him into the chair without pulling Culver from whatever work he's doing to help, so he won't bother with it." Trudy shrugged before taking a sip of her cider. "I think it's his pride that refuses to allow him to ask for help."

Gabriel O'Malley studied the tip of his spoon for a long minute as Fergus at his side, devoured his soup happily.

"How's the strength in his arms?" Gabriel asked her suddenly.

"Quite strong for the most part," she replied.

"What if he could assist you with helping him into the chair?" Gabe asked as an idea blossomed into his head.

"What are ye thinking son?" Fergus asked mid slurp.

"What if there were a rope or a handle that he could use to pull himself into the chair, and all anyone would have to do is positon the seat into the right place for him and hold it steady?"

"Gabe here has a tinker's mind, he does," Fergus informed Trudy proudly. "The boy has built many contraptions about our spread and most of 'em work too."

"It would give him more mobility, but even if we get him in the chair, he'd still be stuck in that room. There's no way to get that chair down the stairs with him in it. It was heavy enough just bringing it up there to begin with, no one will want to trudge it up and down the stairs," Trudy pondered.

"Move his room into the study," Annie remarked quietly as she joined them at the table and began to slice a piece of cornbread for herself. "The room's big enough, and it has a door for privacy."

"It just might work!" Trudy cried out happily.

"Here's what I'm figuring…"

As Trudy listened to Gabriel O'Malley line out a few ideas that had popped into his head, she couldn't help but smile mistily. Mathias Sinclair wasn't going to have any more excuses to close himself off into his room and pretend the rest of the world didn't exist. If Gabriel's contraptions worked, the man would be able to get around and practically care for himself. It would give him so much freedom that soon Mathias wouldn't need her anymore.

-Love blooms when the heart sacrifices-

CHAPTER SEVEN

After seeing the O'Malley men out, their bellies loaded with Annie's potato soup and cornbread, a plan formed between them. Trudy decided that it was time to head upstairs and feed the bear. She'd waited long enough and figured by now he was probably in a sorry need for the chamber pot. If she didn't get to him soon, the man would probably be close to springing a leak. Serves him right with the way he'd talked to her in front of company!

"Mathias I've brought your—" Trudy froze midsentence and nearly dropped the supper tray. All thought that had been formed flew from her mind.

Mathias, stark naked and moaning, had arranged himself upon his side, his bare bottom faced in her direction. Large hands twisting the sheeting into knotted coils, he was in obvious pain. The night shirt he'd previously been wearing lay discarded at the foot of the bed. It was as if he'd tossed it away out of frustration.

"Go away," Mathias growled as he yanked the sheet over his groin to cover himself, but not before Trudy caught an eyeful of taut buttock. Good gravy she thought, who in the world would think a bottom attractive? Yet, there she was admiring his.

"I brought your food," Trudy said weakly.

"Set it down and go," he ordered her through gritted teeth.

"Let me help you," she said closing the door behind her and setting the tray down on the bureau by the door.

"Don't you listen to a thing I say?" Mathias grumbled.

"Not usually," Trudy quipped with a cock of her brow as she approached the bed.

"Trudy, I said go away!" Mathias snapped as he gnashed his teeth, his face and chest glistened with perspiration. "I don't want you around me… not like this."

"Mathias, I'm not leaving you," Trudy informed him as she slipped off her boots and climbed into the bed behind him. Sitting in a ladylike fashion was not going to be a possibility, so Trudy hiked her dress above her knees and knelt next to him.

"You assisted me earlier, now it is my turn to help you."

Lightly running her hand along his spine, she inspected each ridge. Her palms slowly slid lower as she began looking for signs of the knots that she knew formed in his muscles from lying prone for so long.

He groaned against the press of one of her palms, and Trudy knew that she'd found the spot which had been causing him the most discomfort. A few inches lower than his original wound, a small bulge had formed below the skin's surface. Trudy didn't know what to make of it. She'd never seen the like.

"I'm going to try to find some liniment to rub on you," she announced making a move to leave the bed, but he stopped her with his request for her to just continue her light message. Mathias rarely asked for her assistance, so she knew his pain must be great.

After long minutes of Trudy's hands lightly working the muscles of Mathias' back, he finally began to relax his grip on the covers. She could feel the tension ebb from his spine and was glad to be with him in this moment.

"Thank you," he muttered roughly, surprising her with his gratitude.

"I think we should have Doc Fisher out to look at you when he returns from his trip. Maybe he can help find a way to relieve your pain," Trudy suggested. "You refuse to take any of the laudanum that Sebastian had left for you and I'm running out of ideas."

"No more doctors!" Mathias refused.

"Mathias—"

"I said no!"

Trudy said no more on the subject. She wouldn't fight him; it only made Mathias dig his heels in deeper when she did. "Ready to turn over?" she asked. At his reluctant nod, she helped him reposition himself on the bed, before placing an extra pillow beneath his head.

"Annie and I are taking a trip into town the day after tomorrow, do you need anything?" she asked before placing the now less than warm soup tray on the bed next to his feet.

Mathias could tell that he'd hurt her feelings. He was angry at himself for baiting her, but he could not stop himself. Every time she breezed into his room, a sunny smile on her face and hope in her eyes, Mathias felt the craziest urge to shake her. Why couldn't she just leave him be? Why couldn't she just let him die? Instead of obeying his wishes, the woman doggedly returned day after day to push and prod him, and generally make a nuisance of herself. He should have sent her away to begin with, but to his astonishment, he found he couldn't do it.

Mathias looked up into Trudy's face as she busied herself with placing his napkin upon his lap and froze. For a moment her pursed mouth sparked a faint notion in his brain. It was something that he couldn't possibly be remembering, as he knew it hadn't happened. But for some strange reason, Mathias felt as if he'd tasted those pink lips before. It was something only his mind could have conjured, but at that moment he couldn't tear his eyes from her mouth.

Mathias ached to kiss her, to find out if she tasted as sweet as he thought she would. Something within him burned to pull her down to him and explore the feelings stirring within him, to see if he could spark the same heat within her.

He was losing his mind.

Mathias could strangle Fergus and Gabriel both, for planting crazy ideas into his head. If they hadn't gone on about indecency and the like, he wouldn't be having those very same thoughts that he shouldn't be having, about a woman that he shouldn't be having them about.

"Mathias?" she prompted, "Are you ready for it?"

"What?" he gasped. Shaking off his half crazed impulse, he asked "what'd you just say?"

"Your supper," Trudy repeated. "Aren't you ready for your tray?"

"Yes," Mathias exhaled trying to release the tension inside of him.

"I'll leave you to your food," Trudy stated as she struggled to slip her feet back into her boots and walked toward the door. "I think your bath will have to wait until tomorrow."

"Trudy?" Mathias called out halting her.

"Yes?"

"You tell me if anyone is belligerent with you when you go to town," he ordered her.

"Would it truly matter?" she asked him with a wry grin. "I've come to expect it around here, why not there as well?"

"Trudy?" Mathias called out once again as she walked toward the door. What could he say? He couldn't apologize to her. If he did she'd never give up. He needed her to think him heartless and uncaring. He needed her to leave him now, rather than later.

"Is there something else I can do for you?" she asked tiredly, one foot out the door.

"No," he mumbled.

She was worn out and he wouldn't ask her to stay and keep him company just because he didn't want to be alone.

Maybe that bullet had ricocheted into his brain and scrambled it up some? Nothing short of that possibility, could explain his actions since the day he'd woken to find her fast asleep, perched on the edge of his bed. Her hair a mess and her nightdress wrinkled and stained with only God knew what; she had never looked more beautiful to him. All those times that he had seen her in passing, and the few moments that he had taken to flirt with her a bit in town, she had always been perfectly done up. But, seeing her disheveled with dark smudges under her eyes, made her seem more real to him. A pale angel made more human, at least, to his cynical eyes. Of course, when she had awoken a few minutes later, he was pretty darn sure that she was Lucifer in the flesh. That opinion had yet to change.

He had never in his life dealt with a more demanding female, and that included his mother and his little sister Serena, who'd pestered him from the moment she could waddle from her bassinet. Challenging females were nothing new to Mathias. But Trudy... well Trudy brought stubborn to a whole new level.

He just hoped that by the time he sent her packing back to her mother, he wouldn't have killed that spirit that he respected so much.

***

After hours of tossing and turning, Trudy gave up trying to pretend to sleep. She needed to see him, to see for herself that he was all right. That bulge in his spine was really worrying her. She'd only go and check on him, and only stay a moment, she told herself as she threw back the bed clothes.

Grabbing up her candle stub that she'd kept burning by her bedside, Trudy walked to through the short hall toward his room. Taking a deep breath, she turned the knob and tiptoed into the dark room, shutting the door behind her. The draft in the room snubbed the flame, and Trudy gasped.

The moonlight filtering in through the small open window, bathed a slim sliver of light across the bed but offered little illumination in the room. Her eyes were still not accustomed to navigating in the dark as she felt her way to the side of the bed. Trudy winced as she stubbed her bare pinkie toe on the edge of the oak beam that framed the bedstead. The candle fell from her grip as she tried muffling a pain filled cry.

Hopping on one foot, Trudy rubbed her offended toe, doing her best not to utter unladylike utterances as she did so. How could slightly banging the smallest toe on your foot hurt as if you'd rammed your entire foot? Not willing to risk any more of her toes, Trudy's hand went to the bedside table in search of the oil lamp that she knew was positioned atop, intending to light it.

"Leave it," Mathias spoke in the darkness and Trudy shrieked.

Startled, she lost her balance and fell face first across his lap.

"Mathias! Did I hurt you?" she gasped.

"No."

"I am sorry to wake you. I was just checking to see if you needed anything," she explained feeling like a fool for getting caught sneaking into his room like a thief.

"I wasn't asleep. Does your foot hurt still hurt?" he asked with a chuckle as he helped her to sit up, the position seating her across his lap, as if she were a child in need of cuddling. A most indecent cuddle indeed, as his hands went to her hips to still her movements.

"How did you know?" she asked in a whisper.

"Honey, I know everything," Mathias remarked as his large hands roamed the small of her back.

It felt strange to be perched upon him in total darkness, and he doing a kindness for her, but she wouldn't complain. His ministrations felt too good on her sore back so she wouldn't protest. Sweeping the chimney had strained her muscles and she knew tomorrow she'd be cursing his rotten soul for goading her into cleaning it in the first place.

"I should probably light a fire in the hearth for you," she offered with a yawn. As drowsiness washed over her, she laid her head against his chest and snuggled into his embrace. Improper though it was, she needed the comfort tonight. Her nightmares were growing worse.

"It's too warm for a fire."

"After all the trouble I went through?" Trudy gasped in outrage. "You never even wanted a fire?"

Mathias chuckled as she bristled in his arms.

"My enjoyment came from watching you wiggle yourself in there and try to pretend you hadn't gotten yourself stuck."

"You sir are no gentleman!" she admonished, but couldn't help but grin. She wished that she could see his face right then. His amusement even if it was at her expense, was rare.

"Why'd you come to me Trudy?" he asked as he massaged her gently. "What is it you came here for?" Mathias demanded as his hands slid lower over the curve of her bottom.

Her head shot up and her brows rose.

"Mathias that's not my back—" she began to inform him, but his mouth captured hers, stealing her breath.

Shock coursed through her. She was kissing a mad man! One minute he was pushing her away, the next he was pulling her close. As for her, she must have inhaled way too much chimney dust to think straight. Nothing else could explain it, except perhaps she was mad too. Either way, Trudy threw caution to the wind and leaned into him.

Wrapping her arms about his neck, she allowed him to deepen the kiss.

She'd been kissed before, that much was true, but she'd never like this. This was beyond anything that she had ever imagined kissing could be. This was earth shattering!

His lips tore from hers and she nearly pouted until they found purchase on the side of her neck. He nibbled the sensitive path of skin to where it met her shoulder, and Trudy nearly squealed from the wicked sensation rioting through her.

"Mathias," she moaned as one large, calloused palm cupped her right breast and gently squeezed through the material of her faded nightdress.

"I've dreamt about this," he confessed in a whisper against her ear. "About touching you like this."

"*You have?*"

Raking his teeth against the plump lobe, he bit gently and excitement rocketed through her belly. "Do you want more, Sweetheart?"

"Yes," she responded instantly, exposing more of her neck Mathias chuckled deeply before giving her delicate skin more attention.

She knew it was wrong to want him so, but she couldn't help herself.

The scrape of his beard tickled her and she giggled.

"Kiss me," Trudy begged as she pulled gently on a lock of his hair.

"Yes Ma'am," he drawled and Trudy found that she liked him best this way. Doing what she wanted for a change.

Their mouths met once again and his skillful tongue traced the seam of her lips, before delving between them to play with hers. Under her bottom, a hard ridge formed beneath the covers. Though still a virgin, Trudy was not ignorant of its meaning. He wanted her just as much as she him and that thought excited her.

Tearing his mouth from hers, Mathias pressed his lips to her brow and sighed.

"We have to stop now," he panted, "we can't do this Tru."

Trudy nearly cried when Mathias finally put an end to their embrace. She wanted to discover what more could exist between a man and a woman, and she wanted to discover it with him.

"You go on back to bed now," he ordered her gently.

"Mathias," she protested.

"Goodnight Trudy," he said firmly.

Taking her gently by her upper arms, he set her away from him. "Don't come here again like this. Not unless you're willing to leave this ranch, because if you do, I will send you away."

Even though she was unable to see him in the darkness, she had the feeling that he was as serious as a stone. Damn him to hell and back.

***

It was only a few minutes past dawn, but Mathias had not yet been to sleep. The reddish-orange painted sky peeked through the heavy curtains of his room; a testament to the fact that sunrise had indeed begun. Mathias had tried many times throughout the long, empty hours to sleep, but nighttime seemed to bring out the worst in his predicament. At night he was alone, and that was when his mind tortured him the most. Darkness reminded Mathias that he was bed bound… a cold, lonely bed at that, and there was no hope for him. Trudy had probably slept like a baby across the hall just to spite him. Damn her.

He had never expected her to come to him.

When Trudy had first waltzed into his room last night, hopping about like a wounded toad, Mathias had almost sworn that he'd conjured her from his own thoughts. Unbelievably, when she'd fallen into his lap like a present from the heavens, the temptation had been too great. Mathias had taken liberties that he shouldn't have and he'd enjoyed every single one he took. Thankfully he'd stopped himself from going too far and though he hated himself for it, he'd sent her away.

For the hundredth time, he wondered what she would have said, if he'd asked her to stay with him last night. The things he longed to do with her…

A soft knock sounded on his door and Mathias was instantly grateful for the reprieve from his amorous thoughts.

"Come in!" he called out, half hoping it was her unable to sleep; because she was too busy pining for his company, the way he was hers. Not that he would ever admit that thought aloud, and not that she would ever be losing a wink of sleep over the likes of him, but the hope was there.

"Oh," Mathias said evenly as the door opened revealing his early morning visitor. "Come on in Culver."

"Hey boss. Sorry to wake you."

"I was awake," Mathias grunted.

"You in a lot of pain?"

Mathias beckoned his foreman in with a slight wave of his fingers. He was not about to tell the older man the reason that he hadn't slept all night.

Culver entered the room and took a seat in the empty chair that was placed next to the bed. Removing his hat, Culver placed it on his knee and regarded the man that he called friend for so many years.

"I've got a report for you Mathias; you aren't going to like it."

"How bad is it Culver?" Mathias scrubbed a hand over his brow. He knew that if Culver was coming to him, it must be bad.

To say that the Bar S Ranch had been having a run of bad luck was an understatement. Ever since early fall, someone had been deliberately sabotaging Mathias' spread. With each attempt, the perpetrator was becoming brasher and the threats were hitting closer to the main house. After Mathias had been injured in the robbery, it seemed the incidents had stopped for a while, but now they had begun to renew themselves with vigor.

"Besides the poisoning of the water hole a few months back, we've had more fences cut and more than a few head has been stolen." Mathias leaned back in the chair and ran a hand through his hair. "Mathias, it gets worse. More poisoned cattle have been found. A few were even butchered and left to rot. We also found another bottle of Thallium near the new water hole."

"Son of a bitch!" Mathias roared.

The new water hole had been dug closer to the main house, to deter this very thing. A lot of good that had done, Mathias thought with a snort.

"Whoever left it there, didn't get the chance to dump it in. The bottle looks full, so they must have been scared off right quick," his foreman quickly assured him. "I think when we do our hiring next month; we'd better hire double the help. We usually have to fire a third anyway, due to laziness and fighting. As it is, I'm looking to lose Curtis."

"Curtis? What's he done?" Mathias inquired.

"Went on a drunken spree on Friday night at the Rotgut," Culver explained. "He did some serious damage to a table and chairs, until someone managed to stop him. I'm gonna let him go as soon as he sobers up a bit more."

"I keep losing men left and right around this place."

"Hell Matt, the only good one we have right now is Pete, and that isn't really saying much as Pete does more harm than good. We need more men."

"I can't afford to hire more help around here. We have to call in the law now," Mathias said through a clenched jaw.

If he wasn't stuck in this bed, he would be riding out to find the sick bastard who was systematically killing off his herd. He felt worthless. His ranch was under attack, and he could not stand up to fight for all that he had built.

"I hear that Alec Wentworth has appointed his half-brother Hunter, as temporary sheriff. Maybe we better see what he has to say about the situation," Culver agreed.

"I hate having to rely on others," Mathias muttered his fists clenched at his sides. "It's not that I don't like the man, but I have a hard time trusting someone to look after what's mine."

"Well, like it or not, you're going to have to," Culver informed his friend. "You might as well at least get his opinion on the matter."

The foreman grinned suddenly. "You know those boys that grabbed Hunter all those months ago? Well, I hear they are walking a wide path around the new sheriff."

"I can imagine that they would be," Mathias chuckled as he cracked his knuckles. "Those fools picked the wrong man to jump. I think they are lucky that you came up on them that day Culver. If they'd have given the man a chance to fight back, I think it would have been an unfair advantage in Hunter's favor."

"They were reckless kids trying too hard to be men," Culver agreed. "Most of them were too damn afraid of what you were going to do with them to pack up all of their gear when they vacated the bunkhouse."

Mathias had fired the worthless hands that day for their actions, but he'd wanted to tear a strip from their hides as well. He didn't cotton to fools or bullies.

"Do you think it is one of those saddle bums doing this?" Mathias supposed. "Striking back at me out of revenge for my firing them?"

"Could be," Culver agreed tapping a finger on his chin as he considered the possibility. "Somehow, I think there is more going on than just some vindictive cowpokes trying to even the record."

"Whatever is going on around here can't continue," Mathias informed Culver, "if it does, the Bar S might as well go up for auction. I won't be able to make payroll if we lose any more of our stock."

"We'll figure it out," Culver assured him.

-Eventually all secrets spill into the light-

CHAPTER EIGHT

Doctor Sebastian Bixby rubbed his temples with shaking hands and focused once again on the ledgers before him. He hated sums and detested calculating money, which was a good thing, since there was none of that left in the entire vault. There was barely enough in the entire building to cash the payroll of the boys from the Bar S, as they came traipsing in demanding their money.

It was midday morning and though he'd not yet hired a teller to work the front counter, a line had formed of angry citizens wondering why it was taking him so long to complete their transactions. For the hundredth time, he wished Gertrude were with him.

Trudy always had a mind for numbers, and would've made a better banker than he. Trudy had always made a better everything than he.

Anger rolled within him as he thought about how she'd turned her back on her family and left everything to fall on his shoulders. Mother was right, Trudy was plain selfish and didn't deserve his missing her, but he did. For the longest time she'd been his greatest friend and sole confidant, but now he had no one.

He was a doctor damn it! This wasn't supposed to be his responsibility. Sebastian sighed, he was going to have to tell Mother, and he knew it was going to kill her. For the life of him, he couldn't imagine how Joe Vernon could've carried that much money from the bank. It didn't seem possible with as much money as his father had always bragged was within his vault, that one man could have stolen it all.

By the time Sebastian waited on the last man in line, he'd barely a stack of greenbacks and a small pouch of gold dust left. He couldn't afford to open the bank tomorrow unless a miracle occurred and a wealthy patron moved to town wanting to deposit their entire fortune.

What was he going to do?

Bitterly, Sebastian hoped that Trudy was happy, for he sure wasn't. He knew his mother was going to keel over when he told her they were going to have to close the bank and sell the house just to pay back their depositors.

So much for the great and powerful Bixby's! Their papa's legacy was gone and they were paupers. He'd thought they'd known humiliation when Trudy had gone to live on the Bar S, but that was nothing compared to the shame that they were going to have to face when the town found out there was no more money left in any of their accounts.

***

As Annie pulled the buckboard up to the general store, Trudy adjusted the hem of her skirts and prepared to disembark. "I hope that Harlan has enough stock. Your list is a mile long, Annie. He may have a heart seizure," she joked.

"Oh he's used to it," the other woman replied with a smile as she tied the mare to the hitching post and reached into her pocket. Producing a sugar cube, Annie fed the sweet girl the treat before patting her neck. "It'll be

Mathias that'll keel over when he sees the sum of it."

"We just won't show him then," Trudy suggested slyly and together the women burst into the laughter that only co-conspirator's could.

Trudy was so glad that she had gotten to know Annie Culver. The woman was a gem who told Trudy the most amusing stories on their way into town. She'd helped Trudy keep her mind off of Mathias and their ill-fated kiss. That in itself was a miracle, as Trudy thought about how wonderful it had felt in his embrace at least twenty times a day, and she didn't know how to erase it from her mind.

"I'll just bake him a cake and he'll forgive me," Annie, coming up beside Trudy threw an arm about her shoulder and gave a squeeze. "Don't you worry; once the room is finished he'll see it was worth the expense."

Trudy sure hoped so. She didn't want to think what would happen if he was adverse to their surprise.

"Sqaws aren't fit for town." The filthy taunt sounded, interrupting their pleasant mood. "Go on back to where you came from Indian whore. You can leave this sweet little filly with us though; I'm partial to a pale haired gal."

Trudy spun on heel; two young men leaned lazily against the hitching post outside of the general store and leered back at her. She'd seen the men around the Bar S working but didn't know their names or why they were being so cruel.

"How dare you talk to her that way?" Trudy questioned angrily. "She's a lady, and filth like you doesn't deserve to breathe the same air she does."

"What do you know about being a lady?" one of them snickered.

"What is that supposed to mean?" Trudy demanded to know.

"It means," The taller man sneered, "everyone knows you've been tending to more than just the boss's wounds." Nudging his buddy with a grin the man continued, "Isn't that right Toby?"

Trudy gasped at the vile suggestion. She was used to the whispers, but no one had come right on out and said it to her face before.

"Pay no attention to those fools, Trudy," Annie warned in a whisper, "Patrick fired them from the ranch just last night." Grasping Trudy by the arm gently, Annie begged her, "just go on in and give our order over to Harlan. I'll be in as soon as I'm finished picking up that salve for Patrick."

"Not until they apologize," Trudy refused to budge.

"Please Trudy," Annie whispered a thread of fear laced her words. "Just go on in," she begged.

With one final glare toward the disgusting men, Trudy finally nodded. "I'm going."

"She's going, did you hear that Toby?"

"I sure did Curtis."

Sidestepping the harassers, Trudy walked into Harlan's establishment and hoped that Annie quickly followed. She didn't want her friend to be pestered any more by those brutes.

The store was near empty of customers and the owner was just about asleep in the chair that he kept behind his counter.

"Mr. Jones," Trudy greeted him twice before he bothered to open his eyes.

"Why Miz Trudy," he slurred, "How you be?" he asked attempting to stand. The man swayed and caught himself on the counter of his register.

Trudy tried not to roll her own eyes, the man was already drunk. "I've a list for you," she stated before handing it over for his inspection. She hoped to heaven the man wasn't too far gone to fill it.

"Holy!" he gasped. "Miz Trudy, you're buying up my store right from under me. Oh happy day!"

Trudy couldn't help herself she had to laugh at his expression. It was true that to make a room in the study for Mathias they would need many things, but she was hardly buying up his entire inventory.

"Go on Missy and take a look around, you might have missed something! I'll get this tallied up and start loading your wagon," Harlan offered.

"Thank you."

Walking about the store, Trudy headed to a shelf that catered to ladies' needs. She wouldn't purchase anything but she liked to browse the hair combs and whatnot.

She was admiring a set of bone hair pins that Harlan had just gotten in, when she felt a presence behind her.

"Well, well, lookie who's still here Toby," a voice crooned close to her ear. "You looking for somethin' special today?"

Large, filthy hands gripped her hip and drug her closer to a denim clad groin. "I got what you need right here, I can give it to you better than that cripple can," he snickered as he pressed himself against her bottom.

The hair on the back of Trudy's neck rose as repulsion filled her belly. "Let me go!" Trudy hissed as she fought against the tight embrace.

"Maybe you should just let her go Curtis," the weaker Toby suggested obviously not willing to take their nasty little game any further.

"Shut up Toby, don't you see me trying to sweet talk this filly?" Curtis snapped at his friend.

"I don't want to be sweet talked," Trudy muttered through clenched teeth. "I want you to go to perdition!"

"Now that's no way for a lady to talk. I've an idea that'll keep your mouth so busy you won't have time to be sour," Curtis laughed as he spun her in his arms and tried to place his lips upon hers.

Trudy attempted to slap at him but he was stronger than she'd given him credit for. His grip tightened painfully and she yelped just as the bell over the door jingled. Trudy prayed it was Annie.

"Let the lady go!" A voice thundered as heavy steps thumped across the flooring of the mercantile.

"Aw shit, the Injun is gonna do his job huh?" Curtis mocked but did as he was told. "We was just havin' us a bit of fun, weren't we Toby?" he asked his partner.

"The lady doesn't look like she's having any fun," Hunter White-Wolf remarked before turning to Trudy and asking, "Are you alright ma'am?" At seeing Trudy's tentative nod he continued, "If I see you mistreat any lady in my town again," Hunter warned, "I'll treat you to a good ol' Apache welcome, you follow me kid?"

"You think just 'cause your brother made you sheriff, you can tell white folks what to do?" Curtis challenged. "Wasn't too long ago that you was strung up and beaten like one of them Mexican piñatas. It could happen again, Sherriff."

"I'm thinking that you've both got til the count of three to get the hell out of my sight, before I make good on my promise," Hunter warned.

"Come on Curtis," Toby prompted as he pulled on his friend's arm. "Let's go on over to the Rotgut and wet our whistles."

Tense moments passed as the cowpoke tried his best to stare down Hunter, but in the end he must have taken the threat to heart.

"Yeah Toby," Curtis agreed backing down. "This place is beginning to stink up from all these Injuns anyway."

"Apache welcome?" Trudy asked Hunter as the men turned tail and marched through the store.

"It's something not fit for a lady's ears."

"Most don't consider me a lady anymore, so you might as well just tell me," she remarked with a forced laugh.

"Let's just say, it's something that can take long, painful hours and makes a real mess," Hunter replied with a careless shrug.

"Would you have done it to him?" Trudy asked as she rubbed her sore arms. That brute had such a tight grip on her that Trudy was sure she was going to be bruised.

"Probably not. I'm not even Apache," Hunter confessed to her. "My people would dole out far more painful punishments… I would've picked one of those."

"Well, I thank you for coming to my aid and I wish you'd teach me some of those methods for next time, they'd definitely come in handy."

"Ma'am there had better not be a next time."

"Oh Sherriff, with women living like I do, there's always a next time," she informed him wryly. "It's the way of the world."

Before he could comment further the bell over the door signaled another customer entering.

"Trudy!" Annie called out. The poor woman all about ran into a stack of flour sacks so great was her hurry to discover what had happened in her absence. "I saw those lump heads outside crowing about forcing a kiss on you. Did they hurt you?" her friend asked concerned.

"I'm fine. They didn't get what they were after; the Sherriff here prevented them from it," Trudy denied as Annie pulled her into a motherly embrace.

"Praise heaven!"

"I'll see you ladies home," Hunter offered. "I'm thinking those boys are too stupid to heed my advice, and I'd rather not have you both caught unaware."

***

Any appreciative thought that she'd had in regards to the new sheriff showing up and shooing off those ruffians, quickly dissipated upon arrival home.

She'd been ambushed from the moment that she'd shown Hunter White-Wolf up to Mathias' room and it was his entire fault.

"And then the sheriff showed up and that's all there is to the story," Trudy explained for the second time.

"That's all?" Mathias growled. "How can you say that's all?"

Trudy shot Hunter an evil eye as she paced about the room.

Hunter White-Wolf stood off to the side not saying a word in her defense. Oh no, he'd already said enough for Trudy's liking. She'd thought the man was going to just come in and pay his respects to Mathias, she hadn't thought the man would tattle on her. But sure enough, Hunter had turned into quite the gossip, spilling forth every bit of scandal concerning their names.

Trudy had thought that she'd made it clear that she hadn't wanted the tale repeated when they'd arrived at the ranch. Annie who'd agreed albeit reluctantly, went off to bake her promised cake, but the man escorting them had stayed silent. She should have known... Men! They were worse gossipers than women. What was it about menfolk that always had them boasting about their heroics? Trudy had once saved a puppy from being trampled; did anyone see her crowing about it for the last ten years? No, they didn't because; at least she knew how to stay quiet.

"We're getting married," Mathias informed her with a wave of his hand.

"You can't be serious!" Trudy gasped. "That's no solution."

"It's the only solution. It's this or you're going back to town to stay. I won't have anything else happen to you," Mathias demanded firmly.

"I can handle myself in town! This is completely unnecessary and foolish," she argued.

"Handle yourself? Trudy, you were nearly raped by that louse!" Mathias thundered. "It won't happen again. My name will afford you the respect of a married lady. It'll squelch any more talk."

"Bah!" Trudy sputtered. "I'm going to go visit with Annie until you gain your wits again." Turning toward the man standing in the corner trying to cover a grin, she pointed a finger. "And you, Sir," she snapped. "Aren't going to get a single piece of Annie's cake, I promise you that, you…you, talebearer."

Slamming out of the room Trudy left the men to stare after her.

Hunter White-wolf ran a hand over his brow as he stared down at the man reclining in the bed. He'd gotten to know Mathias Sinclair pretty well in the time that he'd been in Liberty. The man still made him a bit uneasy, angry white men had that tendency, but he knew that Mathias was no threat to the woman who'd just stormed off. As the law in these parts, Hunter wouldn't've allowed him to be. Truthfully though, with her temper, Hunter figured he might have to stick around just to protect Mathias from her.

Absently Hunter scratched at the tin star pinned to his shirtfront. It was a sham and he knew it. His half-brother Alec, who just happened to be the mayor, just didn't want Hunter to leave town. So he and the council boys had thrown him a bone. Hunter had reluctantly agreed to fill in as sheriff but only on a temporary basis. In a few months when someone else stepped up to claim the job, Hunter would be out of town faster than a wink of an eye. Until then, he was going to sit back and watch the council lead his brother on a merry chase. It tickled him silly to watch Alec try to outsmart those old fellas.

"How long do you think it's going to take her to realize that you're determined to do this?" Hunter asked with a chuckle.

"I'd give her two hours or so." Mathias suggested dryly.

"That quick huh?"

"It'll have to do," Mathias replied his tone now grave. "As that's about all the time she'll have until you to go fetch Reverend Peterson and get back here."

"I assume I'm invited to the wedding?" Hunter asked his grin widening.

"You'll have to be," Mathias informed him. "I may need you to hogtie the bride."

He owed Mathias Sinclair for saving his life some months back, and Hunter was determined to repay that debt. Even if it meant helping the man tie himself to a woman who'd most likely murder him in his sleep. To each their own Hunter thought with a shake of his head as he headed for the door.

The single men around these parts were dropping off like flies! It was almost as if marriage were catching. Every time Hunter turned around lately another wedding was taking place. He'd better start working on a charm necklace of clove and comfrey to ward off evil spirits least he find himself marching straight into the nuptial noose.

As Hunter left on his mission, Mathias shook his head in wonder. If anyone would've told him four months ago that he'd be marrying Trudy Bixby, he would've laughed in their faces. A woman like her didn't belong with a man like him. He'd nothing to offer her except his name, and like it or not, she was going to take it that very day. He just had to figure out a way to get her to agree.

-A kiss for the bride, sympathy for the groom-

CHAPTER NINE

While the witnesses were smiling, the intended couple wore matching frowns directed at one another.

Trudy wanted to kick every single grinning person in the room. Except Annie, she wouldn't dare do that. But she could glare her into frowning. Yes, Trudy decided, she'd just intimidate the gentle woman into not being so thrilled by her unfortunate circumstances.

"Trudy…" Reverend Peterson called her name, pulling her from her glum thoughts. "I need an answer my dear," he stated kindly.

"Oh! I am sorry sir," she murmured.

Fiddling with the cuff on her brown, hand me down, - uglier- than-sin dress, Trudy fought tears as they gathered in her eyes. This was not how she'd always envisioned her wedding to be.

"Do you take this man as your wedded husband in the eyes of our lord?" the good reverend prompted once again, reminding Trudy of the purpose for his visit today.

"Uhmm—" she stammered.

She was still in shock from the fact that Mathias had Hunter go and fetch the preacher. When Hunter returned, the good Reverend Peterson in tow, she'd been livid. Mathias sensing her heels digging in threatened her with the worst punishment she could think of. He told her that he'd pack her up and send her to live with the most eccentric woman in the territory. Trudy had felt true fear at that moment course through her. She would have agreed to just about anything at that point.

Gertrude Stephens, a woman that Trudy had the misfortune to share a given name with, was crazier than a body had a right to be. There was no way that Trudy was going to be forced to live with Mathias' great Aunt. Trudy knew for a fact, that the woman put baby dresses and bonnets on her legion of cats that roamed her ramshackle mansion and let them lick off of her dishes. Trudy shuddered at the thought of sharing close quarters with one of those beady eyed, rat snatchers of Miss Stephens.' She had about fifty of the blasted furry demons all waiting to pounce on Trudy with their vicious claws. Trudy shuddered at the thought. She wasn't afraid of many things in life. But cats, and living with Miss Stephens, were high on that list of fears.

She had promised to give Mathias' suggestion some thought, but he hadn't given her the time to mull it over. With the preacher at his side, he'd said that it was now or never. She had five minutes to think it over or start packing her bags.

"Trudy," Mathias growled. "Think of the alternative," he'd prompted when she hesitated over her vows.

"I do," she answered in a whisper. Her eyes casted down in shame, she avoided any eye contact with Mathias.

The real truth of why she'd agreed to marry Mathias was because she couldn't bear to leave him. Somewhere along the way she'd fallen in love with the man. It was selfish of her to allow him to do this.

"I now pronounce you man and wife," the reverend spoke quietly. "You may kiss your bride." Closing the heavy bible he held in his hands, the Reverend turned and awaited them to follow his instructions.

"We will pass on the offer," Mathias, her husband now, spoke in a harsh tone and reality crashed down on the nervous bride. There was no going back now. She was married to a man that had no idea just what she'd done, and she had no idea how to tell him. They would be starting a life together based on lies and secrets.

"I would like to congratulate you both on behalf of the entire congregation. I'm sure if circumstances were… ah different, everyone in town would have loved to have been able to attend," Reverend Peterson said in a half convincing lie.

Great! Trudy thought. Lying was catching around this place. The preacher better get out while the getting was good, else his tongue turn to stone.

Sure enough, the town would have loved to have been here, if only to throw rotten cabbages at her head, Trudy thought sourly. She did not have a single friend in this town, at least, not anymore. And the few that she did have before the scandal had long since abandoned her. As he patted Trudy's hand in a gesture of comfort, even the good Reverend was in a hurry to escape the uncomfortable silence in the room.

"Let's go and give the couple some privacy," the preacher prompted with a satisfied voice.

"You don't have to leave!" Trudy all but shouted. So nervous was she to be alone with her new spouse.

As Annie and Hunter followed the man out of the door, Trudy turned to her husband with a scowl that promptly turned to tears at the look of pity on his face.

"Don't you say one word!" she snapped at Mathias as she ran after the others.

***

It wasn't until later that night that Mathias realized that he'd forgotten one important detail when it came to marriage... where his wife would sleep. Of course, Trudy had taken that obstacle out of the way when she'd locked herself in her own room for the night.

Some wedding night that he would be spending!

As Trudy lay beyond the wall in her own bed, he was wide awake and aching. The worst part of it all was that he longed to call out to her, if only to have her sit beside him on the bed. Mathias knew if he'd chosen to, Trudy would have come running as fast as possible and care for his every need. That fact made him feel both angry and inadequate.

And now... now he'd gone and married his sweet tormenter. Instead of scaring Trudy off like he should have done months ago, he'd gone and given the woman his last name.

Mathias sighed as he focused his attention on the far wall. The barrier stood mocking him, reminding him that he couldn't touch his bride. It was probably for the best anyway. He wanted her to want to be here, not because she felt obligated to him for taking that damn bullet for her, and not because he'd forced her to. He cursed himself for the fool he was. He was once again back to wanting a woman who he could never be worthy enough for.

Trudy was too good for the likes of a crippled man with more debt than noble qualities. She was meant to be a rich man's bride. Not meant to waste her youth caring for a pathetic invalid. She knew it too. There was a reason the woman had burst into tears at the thought of marrying up with him.

It was just like when he'd asked Daisy Lynn to marry him all those years ago; he had nothing to offer his new bride. Trudy was no Daisy, the last month had proved that, but how long would it be until she found herself unhappy and longed to wander?

At least all of those years ago he could have given his bride a night that she would never have forgotten. Once again, Mathias cursed his useless body, as he looked down at the tent of sheeting on his lap; he knew it had cursed him right on back.

***

"Patrick," Annie Culver turned over in bed and shook her husband's arm.

"Hm?" he mumbled.

Turning his large, muscular body toward hers; Patrick placed an arm about her naked waist and pulled his wife closer to his warm body.

"Are you asleep?" Annie asked him.

It was a silly question she knew, for he'd been snoring for some time now. "I'm sorry to pester you," she whispered.

"I'm up," he said with a yawn before kissing her bare shoulder. "Is it another bad dream?"

Patrick had always been like that. Instead of grouching at her for waking him as most men would, Patrick would instantly reach out to comfort her. He'd always put her first in the many years that they'd been married, almost to the extreme. Sometimes it irritated Annie when he treated her as if she were a frayed rope, ready to snap at any moment.

"No. It's not a bad dream," Annie admitted.

"What's the matter?" Patrick sat up instantly concerned. Light flickered as he struck a match and lit the stub of a candle on his side of the bed. "Is your head paining you again?"

"I am fine. I just can't sleep."

The sheet falling to his lap afforded his wife a good eyeful of manly flesh in the dim lighting. Annie grinned in appreciation. Her man was one finely built warrior. The battle scars he carried puckered white upon his sun browned skin. In the nearly twenty years that they'd been married, Patrick's body had yet to fall soft around the middle as most men his age had. As always, Annie's mouth watered at the sight of him.

"So, it's another round of loving that you're wantin,' Annie girl," Patrick said with a wicked grin as he caught the lust that lingered in her gaze. "Well let's get a move on then Sweetheart. The rooster crows too early around this spread," Patrick chuckled as he pulled her slim body on top of his.

Only a few short hours before, he had pleasured her until she'd cried out for mercy; she should be dead to the world. Even though Patrick had nearly worn her out, Annie found herself unable to sleep. Her mind continued to race.

"Patrick," Annie sighed as his hands roamed her bottom. "I want to talk to you about Trudy," she protested weakly as he began to suckle at her naked breasts.

"Hmm," he grunted obviously ignoring the topic.

"Patrick! I'm talking to you," Annie rapped him on the forehead lightly, yet hard enough to get his attention.

"Hey now!" Patrick Culver's jaw dropped. It wasn't like his wife to distract him from making love to her, let alone lift her hand to him, even playfully.

"Pay attention to me," Annie snapped sternly.

"I thought I was!" When she made a move to rap him once again for his impertinence, he caught her hand in his. "What about her?" he asked gruffly, rubbing his offended head.

His concentration had been focused on more important matters at that moment, and he honestly couldn't care less about the boss's new bride.

"She doesn't think you like her," Annie informed her husband.

"I don't," Patrick stated baldly.

"Why not?" Annie asked aghast. "She is lonely and needs a friend or two."

"Lonely?" Patrick snorted.

"She has done nothing but help Mathias since she came here," Annie said, her tone becoming hard. "No one in town will even speak to her because of it."

"Annie," Patrick exhaled. Sitting up fully in the bed, he wrapped Annie's legs about his waist and kissed her chin. Catching her jaw between his wide palms, Patrick looked into her beautiful dark eyes for a moment before he finally spoke. "Listen to me. That woman is the reason that Mathias is trapped in that bed to begin with. She is spoiled and not someone you should concern yourself with."

"That's not true Patrick," Annie snapped. "The reason Mathias can't walk is because that evil Joe Vernon shot him. Trudy had nothing to do with the robbery."

"Trudy hm?"

Patrick sighed. His wife had obviously already made up her mind to befriend the woman… and now she was going to work on her husband until she convinced him to do the same.

It wasn't going to happen.

Patrick would not stand by and watch his friend be led around by the nose by a pretty face like he had when Mathias was slobbering over Daisy Lynn. Back then Patrick had kept his opinions to himself, figuring that Mathias was a grown man who knew his own mind. But now, Mathias was more vulnerable, and come hell or high water, he wasn't going to let another woman ruin his friend.

"Patrick, we need to help her."

"What's on your mind darlin'?" he asked with a groan.

Patrick would rather just make love to her until she couldn't think straight instead of discussing his friend's new marriage, but Annie was hell bent on talking. And when Annie was hell bent on talkin' then Patrick was better off listening to what she had to say. At least he'd better, if he didn't want to spend the night out on the front porch sleeping with his old, gaseous dog, Beaux.

"I think she will be good for Mathias," Annie declared with a firm nod. "Just give her some time and you'll see."

"Don't go getting any ideas about matchmakin' Annie," Patrick warned. "Married folks have got work out their problems for themselves."

"Sometimes folks just need a little bit of a push to get things started," Annie argued.

"Better be careful Sugar," Patrick warned. "Matchmakers around this part usually end up paying the price."

"And what price would that be?" Annie asked archly.

"This price!"

Within seconds, Annie found herself flat on her back, with her husband plastered over her. Sighing in pleasure, Annie thought that paying the price had never been so sweet. As his mouth teased about her ribs, she giggled. What a wonderful price to be paid indeed…

-Strength grows when love is shown-

CHAPTER TEN

George Sinclair studied the young woman sitting by his bedside. His wife was over joyed by the news that the slim girl had brought them today, but George was not so easily fooled. Trudy Bixby, now Sinclair, was not the picture of a happy new bride.

"I cannot believe I missed another one of my children marrying! This is just beyond words!" Charlotte exclaimed. "I am so happy that you have joined our family Trudy, but why didn't you wait until we could be in attendance? We would have—"

"Charlotte," George cut Charlotte Sinclair off before she further upset the young woman. "Could you please fetch me a bite to eat?" he asked his wife trying to distract her.

Charlotte, stunned that George was actually asking for food, sat with her jaw slackened. George knew her shock was due to the fact that he hadn't had much of an appetite in the last few weeks. He had tried to fool her into thinking that he was eating more than he was, but Charlotte was not easily deceived. He knew that she was worried, and in doing so, Charlotte was wearing herself out trying to control the situation. She was losing weight and dark circles marred her beautiful eyes. Charlotte just didn't grasp the concept that she couldn't control everything; she was too hardheaded, much like their son.

Death was coming for George, there was no doubt in his mind that it would be sooner rather than later, but he wasn't ready to go just yet. George had made peace with his past and the things that he'd done in his youth, he knew he was forgiven for his sins and missteps. The time when he'd been young and idealistic, seemed so very long ago. He needed to make sure that charlotte and the children would be all right, and then he could die in peace.

As soon as Charlotte flew from the room, George turned to his new daughter by marriage. "Are you well Trudy?" he asked her.

"I am sir," she said gracing him with a ghost of a smile.

"I cannot help but notice that you seem uneasy dear. Is there something on your mind that you need to air? I'm a good listener."

"Mr. Sinclair, I—"

"George, call me George," he encouraged her with a smile. "After all, we are family now."

"George, I tried to talk your son out of this whole debacle. I truly did," Trudy informed her new father in law. "He is so stubborn that—"

"If Mathias married you, then it was because he had a good reason to. I know my son. He is so bull headed, that he can't be told what to do," George assured her. "Give him time. He will come around. You're a good girl Trudy and I think you'll make an excellent wife for my son."

"I feel as though I am just burdening your son even more so than he already was," Trudy confessed. "I don't think that I am fit for the life of a rancher's wife."

"Fit?" George cocked his head. "Why do you find yourself lacking young lady?"

"I can't ride. I am more accustomed to tea socials and ordering servants than I am herding cattle."

"Herding cattle!" George exclaimed before laughing. "Darling girl, no one expects you to do anything more than be yourself."

"That's not true. Annie can do everything. She bakes, she can shoot a deer and dress it... please don't ask how I know that," Trudy said with a shudder at the memory of watching her do it a few months ago. "I can't even manage the work on day," she confided.

"Annie knows what Annie has been taught," George said gently. "You just need to find a few simple things that you are able to do around the ranch. Soon enough you will prove to everyone including yourself just what you're capable of," George encouraged her.

"Enough of my troubles," Trudy announced with a forced smile.

Pulling a cloth wrapped bundle from her reticule she announced, "I've brought you some of those peppermint candies that you hide under your pillow from Charlotte."

"Quickly! Pass them over before she comes back," George said excitedly.

Charlotte in actuality couldn't care less if he had the candies, but it had begun to become a game between him and his wife. Charlotte would catch him sneaking a candy and demand he hand his stash over. For every candy that he produced, she would reward him with a kiss. The next morning, a small pile of candy would appear on his breakfast tray, a sure sign that she enjoyed the game as much as he did. God, but he loved that woman.

Later as Trudy went to leave, George stopped her. He had something that he wanted the young woman to hear before she left. Time was short for him and he knew that if he needed to say something, he'd better get to it or it would never be said.

"Trudy," he began tiredly. "Listen to me. I want you to know that not many people would have had the courage or the knowledge to save my son's life."

"That was Sebastian's doing sir, I only helped him."

"You need to have faith in yourself, Trudy," George said squeezing her hands in his. "Remember that you are stronger than you give yourself credit for."

Taking a worn bible from the table by his bedside, George pulled a folded slip of paper from within.

"Trudy," George said quietly. "I'm dying."

"Oh, George—"

"Please, after I'm gone can you give this letter to Mathias for me? You'll know when the time is right."

"Of course." Trudy took the paper with a sad smile. "But you're going to be able to give this to him yourself. I know it."

"Just be good to him Trudy, and trust that he will come around," George begged. "In the meantime, go on home and give him hell. A man needs a good woman in his life that can give him a healthy dose of trouble... keeps our blood pumping."

"Thank you," she mumbled.

Rising, Trudy held his hand in hers; he could see the tears in her eyes that she was trying not to show. George gave hers an affectionate squeeze before she took her leave. She was brave this woman that his son had decided to marry.

George watched her go with a sad smile. How in the world had a self-righteous prig like Thomas Bixby created such a spitfire? Trudy reminded him much of his own Charlotte once upon a time. He would probably burn in hell for thinking it, but he was glad that Thomas was dead. That way he had no more sway over the girl. A daughter deserved every happiness in the world, and should be treasured. Thomas Bixby hadn't known that his true wealth was within the children he and Edna had created, and George felt sorry for him.

Something told him that while Trudy had never been shown her value, she would soon come to understand her worth. It was too bad he wouldn't be around to see the children that Mathias would create with her. They were going to be hellions just like their parents, he thought with a smile.

***

Four days later, Trudy sat by her husband's side on his new bed. The early spring air wafted through the open window and into the room ruffling his hair. Trudy itched to reach out and smooth the stray lock that had fallen over his brow.

"You don't like it do you?" Trudy said with a pout as Mathias sat in silence. They had all worked so hard on decorating his room to surprise him and it was disappointing that he didn't care for it.

Gabriel had come just that morning and installed his rope and pulley mechanisms. With the help of his two younger brothers, Gabe had tested them for safety and worked out any issues. While the boys did that, Annie helped Trudy hang the new lacy curtains that they'd sewn. Fergus O'Malley not wanting to be left out of the excitement had done his duty by sitting perched on a chair and giving orders to his younger grandsons on how to arrange the furniture about the room. Even Culver had lent a hand and built the large square frame that the new, bigger bed rested upon.

"There's no fireplace in here, but I'm sure we will still be comfortable..." Trudy trailed off as his head shot up and their eyes met.

"You want to share this room?" he asked her as if he hadn't heard her explanation for the mechanism.

"I am your wife," Trudy laughed hollowly. She wasn't going to beg him to make love to her, but she was sure going to throw a little of a hint his way.

Licking her lips nervously, she tried to smile reassuringly. "Once you get used to the rope pull, you'll have much more strength to get about."

Mathias eyed the contrivance with a measure of doubt. The blasted thing looked like something out of a nightmare. But even the fear of the thing collapsing on him and killing him wasn't what held him in awkward silence. His pride warred with his shame as he realized that he owed Trudy a debt of gratitude. She'd worked hard to make a lovely room for him and he'd been nothing but a stubborn ass to her for so long.

"Thank you," he managed and was stunned at how easy it was to make her happy. The blinding smile she gifted him had him clearing his throat in embarrassment.

Marriage was harder than Mathias had thought it would be. He should've had his head examined instead of taking those vows. One week married, and still they hadn't addressed the elephant in the room, consummating their marriage. Trudy had remained sleeping in the small room just as before, but he knew she kept hinting at wanting to join him. Mathias was at a loss as to what to do. Well, he knew what he wanted to do, he just didn't know if his body would let him.

Lifting her small palm into his hand, Mathias pressed it to his chest. He had to find a way to explain it to her, without disgusting her or embarrassing her. It wasn't that he didn't want her, he truly did, he just didn't know if he could want her, not in the way a husband wanted his wife, and that wasn't fair.

"Trudy, I think we should—"

"Knock, knock," Alec Wentworth lightly pounded on the door with a laugh. "I've come a callin' and you'd better be dressed," he joked as he opened the door and froze at the sight of Mathias holding her hand.

Grabbing her hand back, Trudy rose from the bed and greeted their guest.

"I'll let you men visit, I'm needed in the kitchen anyway," she informed them. "Mathias, we'll talk later?"

At his nod, she fled the room before he could tell her that he didn't want her sleeping by his side.

"Well, well, well… look who's the one playing loosey goosey with a woman he shouldn't. Guess I'm not the only rogue about the place anymore," Alec chuckled merrily.

"Shut your trap it's not what you're thinking," Mathias snapped as the fool grinned slyly in his direction.

"Oh really? It sure looks like I interrupted something interesting. I'm guessing that nurse of yours was thinking it was something curious too, judging by the blush on those cheeks of hers."

"That's my wife you're talking about you ass," Mathias said, his temper starting to flare.

"What!?"

"We were married a few days ago," he informed Alec grimly.

"Married?" Alec, Mathias's new brother-in- law and ex best friend, sputtered.

Mathias wished for the tenth time in the last quarter of an hour, that his wife hadn't admitted the man into his sickroom. But Trudy, being Trudy, had never followed his wishes to be left alone.

"Yes," Mathias answered with a shrug. "I am surprised that the news isn't all over town by now."

"Married? You actually married her?" Alec howled in laughter and Mathias felt his temper rise. "She must do some wonderful nurturin' to prompt a confirmed bachelor such as you into stepping inside the parson's trap."

Mathias could not say just exactly what prompted him to plant his fist into Alec's belly, but he did it. Trudy was a pain in his hind end, that much was true, but she was his pain in the ass and he wouldn't stand for anyone to mock her.

After Alec finished wheezing and dry heaving, he glared at Mathias. "Wait until Serena hears about this. You know that those two hiss and scratch at each other like angry barn cats."

"My sister has nothing to say about my choice in bride. Trudy and I have an understanding that no one need concern themselves with," Mathias said harshly. "Serena didn't ask my opinion before she chose to mate her life to yours, so she can hold onto her own thoughts."

"Oh?" Alec eyed Mathias with a gleam in his eye. "Just what do you have going on between the two of you?"

"Let's put it this way," Mathias said grinning suddenly. "Trudy has learned a few lessons in how to take care of a jolly fellow such as myself."

"Good lord, I actually feel sorry for Trudy," Alec said shaking his head. "She really isn't a bad sort Mathias. I hope you're not being cruel to the girl."

"Enough. Stay out of my marriage and tell me about yours. Is my sister happy?" Mathias asked changing the subject. "I might be confined to this bed, but I will find a way of beating the daylights out of you, if Serena so much as sheds a single tear because of you."

"Oh she cries alright, but it is in ecstasy…"

Luckily, Alec dodged the fist that was headed its way back toward his mid-section.

"Why don't you come a bit closer so I can lay you out flat?" Mathias offered his friend, his eyes narrowed.

"Not on your life. You might throw that pan of water on me and ruin my new suit," Alec suggested with a nod toward the basin on the bedside table. He brushed an imaginary wrinkle from his lapel. "Can't have such quality material ruined, it would be a travesty."

"As if I would waste my bathwater on the likes of you, Trudy would have to trudge in more, and she spills half of it on the way," Mathias grumbled. "As it is, she takes forever just getting half a pan of it in here."

"So Trudy, uh, helps you does she?" Alec's brow rose and he smirked.

"Well I can't very well walk to the bathing closet now can I? Trudy just gives me a hand is all."

"Lucky dog," Alec said with a laugh. "You've just given me the idea of a delightful way to spend the afternoon with your sister!" Pulling a tightly bundled deck of cards from his vest pocket, Alec tossed them to his friend. "Here, I'll return the favor."

"What's this?"

"It's just a little something to keep you and the Missus busy. I suggest you teach her how to play poker. It can be very…rewarding." Laughing, the mayor headed toward the door.

"What's so amusing?" Mathias demanded confused.

"You'll figure it out."

Turning, Alec grinned widely and wished the newly wedded Mathias a happy marriage bed. As Alec exited the room, he pretended that he hadn't seen the crude gesture that Mathias made in return.

***

"Are you leaving so soon Mayor Wentworth?" Trudy greeted Alec as she passed the finely dressed gentleman in the wide hallway. She held a lap tray loaded down with Mathias' lunch and frowned as the mayor snatched a honeyed tea biscuit. Annie had helped her bake those especially for Mathias. The hope was to sweeten his sour mood toward Trudy through his stomach, and Annie had been busy this morning trying to teach Trudy how to bake a proper treat. It had taken four batches before Trudy had gotten the hang of it, now they were in short supply of molasses, Trudy could not afford to lose a single one of Mathias' favorite treats.

"Don't go back in there," Alec Wentworth warned her. "Mattie boy is in a foul temper. You're better off heading into town for a day of shopping and jabber jawin' than sitting in there with that stubborn mule," he joked as he bit off a hunk of his pilfered booty.

"And miss his grouching? Oh dear, the loss of amusement would just break my little ole' heart," Trudy quipped sassily, as she moved her tray to evade his hand, as it reached for another sweet biscuit. She refused to lose another to his greedy paws.

"How is your mother settling in? And your brother, how is he adapting to his new position?" Trudy asked politely. "I never got a chance to thank him for something he did for me recently."

Truthfully, she found it hard to make idle conversation when the tray was growing heavier by the moment, and she was in a hurry to watch Mathias' surprise as he learned it was she, not Annie, that had baked his favorite treat. But, Trudy was turning over a new leaf. Nothing short of the Lord above was going to stop her from becoming a better person. So, Trudy was resigned to feigning interest despite the ache in her arms.

"Mother is being courted by Doc Fisher, now that he is back in town to stay. I see him more at my house these days than I do of Hunter. Which is the better end of the deal in my opinion," Alec said with a wink. "But I'll pass your thanks along."

"Please do that, he's definitely a wonderful addition to our town."

"We are definitely a growing town," Alec agreed. "But I wouldn't go calling Hunter wonderful."

She'd forgotten that Alec still wasn't too thrilled to find out he had a brother.

"Giving you problems is he?" Trudy asked with a grin.

"Hunter has stepped in just fine as sheriff. There hasn't been too many grumbles from the people as of yet. But give the boy some time; he has a way of rubbing people the wrong way," Alec chuckled.

Trudy knew that Hunter had a hard row to hoe ahead of him. As a half Indian, half white man, he had some prejudice in store for him. Though the people of Liberty, Texas, prided themselves on their forward thinking and progressive theories, they were still a mixture of hodgepodge individuals. Some good, some bad, and sadly some that would never view Hunter as their equal. Those few that saw the color of his skin and not the value of his soul, would try to make trouble for him. Some Christians seemed to forget the teachings of the book that they so highly praised. They'd certainly been quick to condemn her.

Her papa had been much the same. Although, Thomas Bixby tended to look down his nose at pretty much everyone but himself and his only son Sebastian. His daughter and his very own wife had been found lacking in Thomas' eyes.

Trudy thought of her brother and her stomach knotted. She missed him so much and worried that he wasn't taking care of himself. Had his tremors lessened or only gotten worse?

"Sebastian must be grateful that there is a second doctor in town to help with his load. How many towns can boast of two doctors?" she remarked.

"I'm guessing you don't know."

"Know what?" Trudy asked him.

"Sebastian gave up his practice; he's been over at your father's bank each day trying to get a handle on running the bank."

"I didn't know, thank you."

Poor Sebastian he'd never had a head for figures. By week's end he'd be batty.

"Well," Trudy said brightly. "Give my regards to your wife." Trudy was proud that she didn't choke on those words. See? A person really could be good if they wanted to…couldn't they?

"Will do," Alec said inclining his handsome, auburn head. "Well, welcome to the family Mrs. Sinclair. Let me know if there is anything I can do to help with Mathias," Alec said in a somber tone. "If you need anything at all, Serena and I are here for you."

"Thank you," Trudy managed around the lump that formed in her throat. "I will keep that in mind."

"Well I must be off now! Serena has surely been missing me by now," Alec said with a wink as he practically danced down the hallway and through the foyer.

"Goodbye!" Trudy called after him, but she knew that his mind was too wrapped up in thoughts of his wife to pay her any notice.

What a joy it must be to marry for love. Serena Sinclair had been blessed, and Trudy just hoped that the red headed menace appreciated her good fortune.

With a sigh, Trudy adjusted the tray in her grip and continued her walk toward her husband's room. Balancing the tray awkwardly, she managed to single handedly turn the knob and push the door open with her foot. Entering the room she watched as her husband shuffled a deck of cards in his hand.

"I've brought you something sweet," she announced.

Happy that by a blessed miracle she'd kept the mayor from devouring them all on the way in there, she displayed her goods.

"Have you now?" Mathias asked as he cut the deck once again and palm shuffled the cards at random.

"What are those for?" she asked as he eyed her sheepishly.

"I think I'm just starting to figure that out."

-Daring can lead to great things-

CHAPTER ELEVEN

Trudy placed her cards down with a groan. She was horrid at this game and she didn't like it at all, but it amused Mathias to watch her lose, so she humored him. On their first night together sharing a bed, she hoped that she could do more than just amuse him at cards.

"Well," Mathias crowed, "looks like I won again!"

"A gentleman would let a lady win a hand or two," Trudy informed him with a sniff.

"My dear wife, when did you start considering me a gentleman?" he joked as he began shuffling the cards once again.

"I don't want to play anymore."

"What do you want to play?" he teased as she pouted playfully.

"I'm tired of games," Trudy announced as she rose from her seat and walked to the door. Slipping the lock in place, she leaned against the door. "I have something else in mind," she announced with a wicked gleam in her eye.

"What's going on in that pretty head of yours?" Mathias asked with a grin.

Trudy was filled with an equal mixture of hope and false daring. She was an accomplished flirt, but could she be an accomplished seductress as well?

"I think you know what I'm thinking," she whispered before nibbling her bottom lip.

"Tru—"

"Don't," she begged, holding one palm outward. "Don't say a word unless it's what I want to hear."

Long minutes passed in awkward silence before Mathias gave a brief nod. Stacking his hands behind his head, he lay back against the mountain of pillows, his expression solemn.

"Unbutton your top," Mathias ordered her gently.

Trudy hesitated a brief moment before obeying his demand. With shaking fingers she released the buttons at her neck and allowed the material to part slightly.

"Not enough," he said with a shake of his head. "Bare your breasts for me."

"Mathias—" she squeaked nearly losing her nerve.

"You wanted to play this game Trudy; so it is up to you to call a halt to it."

Trudy knew that her cheeks must be flaming red by now, but she was not going to lose heart.

Pulling her arms from the nightdress, Trudy bared herself to him. The cool breeze from the window blew across the tips of her nipples, tightening them, and she whimpered.

Mathias' eyes devoured her but he gave no indication that he wanted more from her.

"What do I do now?" she asked unsure.

Crooking a finger, he gestured for her to come to him.

Her bare feet sauntered across the wooden planks of the floor softly until they came up against the side of the bed.

"Take the rest of the gown off," Mathias demanded gravelly.

She stood proudly before him and dropped the garment to the floor and the air in his lungs was stolen from him.

Her breasts, small and firm, would fill his palms nicely. The tightened pink nipples cresting them were the most enchanting shade of rose that he'd ever the privilege of viewing.

"Mathias," she whispered and shifted. He could tell that she was uncomfortable with his scrutiny, but he couldn't drag his eyes from the indulgence before them.

The sweet indent of her navel drew Mathias' attention as she inhaled another deep breath. Mathias nearly swallowed his tongue in desire, as his eyes traveled downward until they feasted on the small pale triangle of curls that shielded her feminine core. She was every sexual fantasy that he'd ever had, combined into one perfect vision. Just the sight of her, and Mathias felt himself harden.

"Come here Trudy," Mathias ordered roughly.

"Why?" Trudy shook her head. "You are just going to push me away like you always do." She stooped to pick the discarded gown from the ground, but did not don it. She still stood exposed before Mathias and refused to show him just how much his rejection would hurt her should he choose to do so.

"I said come here."

Mathias held his hand out and after a few tense moments, she took it. Climbing into the bed beside him, she tossed the gown away from her and allowed her naked flesh to press against his. Trudy lay with her head on his chest and listened to the rapid beat of his heart.

"So, you want to become a real wife? You want me to take you?" Mathias couldn't help himself; he leaned down and kissed the top of her beautiful head. He ran his hands down her bare back, tracing the sweet curve of her spine, until he could palm a handful of her delightful buttock.

"Do you really know what you want?" He asked her quietly. "You think letting me rut with you is the way to make this work? Do you honestly think that sex can change our situation?" Mathias chuckled dryly. "Honey, you're not putting enough worth onto yourself."

"I want you Mathias. Right or wrong, I want to be a good wife to you."

"Trudy, your virginity is a gift. Don't give it to me out of a sense of gratitude for my taking that bullet," he warned.

"Mathias Sinclair, I am getting plain tired of you insisting that I don't know my own mind. And, if you don't make love to me, I am going to scream this house down.' Trudy huffed. Rising up on her elbow she poked one finger into the hard planes of his stomach and narrowed her eyes. "Honestly, you're the most hardheaded man that I've ever known!"

"I'm worried honey," Mathias said in a moment of pure honesty. It was hard to admit the truth, but she deserved it. It may take him a moment to swallow his ego, but he was going to lay bare what kept him from taking all she had been offering him.

"What is it? What's wrong?" Trudy looked into his eyes, and saw the burden he carried but was unable to share. "Tell me Mathias; no matter what it is I can help."

"I am worried that I can't be the man you need... in that way. I won't be able to pleasure you. Not like I would have, before the shooting."

"I know you can become...um..." Trudy waved a hand toward his lap and bit her lip.

"Aroused yes, I can become aroused. Thankfully that hasn't been affected!" Mathias laughed at her blush.

"Then what is the problem?" Trudy bravely inquired. "Tell me," she prompted, when he remained silent. He stared at her, as if trying to record her every feature to memory.

"I feel like half a man! Why can't you understand that woman? Why!" Mathias thundered and regretted the outburst immediately as she shied away from his anger. "I'm sorry Trudy. You know that I would never hurt you, don't you?"

"Mathias, look at me," Trudy tenderly cupped the side of his face. She was not afraid of the large man stretched out next to her. It was just instinct to move herself out of hitting range. His temper may flare every now and then, but she knew that it was from frustration, and that he would never strike her. Trudy knew she was always safe with him. He would never lift his hand to her as her papa and mama always had. He had always been gentle and kind in the past to her. Unfortunately, the day of the robbery had changed everything this man believed about himself. He saw himself as a shell, as less than masculine. She saw him in a completely different light. Trudy saw him as he was before, proud, handsome and a hardheaded cuss of a man.

Turning his stubborn jaw until their eyes met, she whispered to him. "You can never be half a man Mathias, never to me."

Trudy bit her tongue from telling him what lay in her heart. Trudy knew that she loved him and always would, but she was afraid to admit it. Frightened to say the words aloud and have him scoff or worse yet, pretend he felt the same as to not hurt her feelings.

"We're going to make love tonight Mathias," Trudy insisted. "And if you ask nicely, I promise I'll even be gentle with you."

"Minx," he chuckled before lightly pinching her bottom.

"You will have to do most of the work," he warned, as dark desired swirled in the depths of his eyes.

"Just show me. Show me how to love you," Trudy replied with a compassionate smile. "I promise to pay close attention."

"Come here woman and kiss me," Mathias growled playfully as she hurried to comply with his demand.

As their lips met in rush of need, Mathias wrapped her fully into his embrace. He traced the seam of her lips with his tongue, prompting her to open for him. Deepening the kiss, Mathias wished that he could roll her beneath him and bury himself inside her luscious body. Unfortunately, any movement caused pain to shoot down his useless legs, and his body would lock up. Not conducive for a man trying to make love to his wife for the first time. The last thing he needed was to end up screaming in agony atop his frightened, naked, wife. Just his luck, they'd have to shout the house down in order to get help to get him off of her.

"You'll have to come on top of me," Mathias instructed as he reluctantly drug his mouth from hers.

"On top?" Trudy asked unsure.

"Trust me honey," Mathias said with a slow grin. "You'll understand in a minute."

Trudy hesitated for a moment, but then with his help climbed in the position that he'd requested. Her body poised astride him, she closed her eyes and allowed herself to just feel his body beneath hers. The strength of him, coupling with her softness, was a heady mixture.

"You're so beautiful Sugar," Mathias proclaimed.

Her knees spread on either side of his hips, Trudy felt her cheeks heat in embarrassment as she realized just how exposed her body was to him. She felt his hands cup her aching breasts and sighed as his large thumbs gently caressed her peaked nipples.

"Mathias," she moaned as he applied more pressure.

"There's more," he promised as one hand traveled down the path of her belly to the juncture of her thighs.

As Mathias' fingers stroked the soft folds of her sex, Trudy moaned low in her throat. She never imagined how wondrous it would feel to be so intimate with him. Her hips rocked against him out of instinct, as she tried to find relief to the ache building between her thighs. She was too shy to voice her need, not that she understood it as it was.

Taking himself in hand, he guided his swollen member slowly into her warmth. She was heaven, pure heaven wrapped tightly around his hard flesh.

"Mathias!" Trudy squeaked as he gripped her hips and pulled her slowly down further onto his rock hard staff. It was his turn to groan low in his throat, as she gloved him fully. The fragile barrier of her virginity gave, and was no more. There was something breathtaking and poignant in joining his body to hers. It was more than just lust in that moment… it was something close to healing.

"I can't!" Trudy gasped, and tried to pull away from him.

"Relax Tru," he whispered huskily. "Let me guide you."

At her tentative nod, Mathias began to stroke his palms over the velvety skin of her back, until he felt her muscles uncoil. With each caress she began to shift her hips in response, seeking more of his touch. Her body so new to lovemaking moved in pure feminine instinct atop him.

"Kiss me," he entreated as he pulled her torso flush with his so that he could capture her lips. The movement allowed Mathias to sink deeper into her tight passage as she rocked gently upon his staff. His hands gripped her hips and he hoped that he could last long enough to bring her to fulfillment.

After, as she lay in his arms sleeping soundly, Mathias relived the act in his mind. Every touch, every sigh that she had made was humbling. No other woman had brought him to such heights before. With Trudy, he had barely held onto his control. Her passion and grace was unbelievably sexy to him, but it was more than that. The woman both angered and amused him, with her ways. Everything about Trudy pushed and prodded at his shell, forcing him to open up and allow her in. Mathias didn't know how he felt about it, but he knew he wanted more from her.

Kissing her bare shoulder, Mathias pushed away a strand of her pale hair that had fallen in her face. She was beautiful, almost angelic in rest, and Mathias felt himself stir once again. Arousal coursing through him, he pulled his hands from her tempting flesh, and dared not awaken her.

As he found himself drifting off to sleep, for the first time in many months, Mathias found himself at peace.

***

"Sebastian, don't be a fool!" Edna snapped as she paced about their parlor in her nightclothes. Her hair twisted in rags, she looked akin to the Greek monster Medusa. "We can't tell these people that their money is gone."

"We can't hide it either Mama," Sebastian said wearily. "People are bound to notice that they only money that's being paid out are the small deposits that are coming in."

"We just need to buy a little more time," Edna pleaded. "I know that your father was working on a few foreclosures before he died, with the sale of those properties, we will have enough to stay afloat."

"Mama…"

Sebastian pinched the bridge of his nose and prayed for the patience that he'd need to make it clear to his mother.

"What if we found the money that Vernon took?" Edna asked a gleam of hope in her eyes.

"How are we going to find the money that everyone in the territory seems to be looking for?" Sebastian asked her gently.

"We know that boy's body was found real close to the Bar S," Edna smiled. "No one has been given permission to search the land. If you remember son, the horse Joe Vernon was riding that day was stolen from Sinclair himself. It stands to reason that the money would be on Sinclair's land."

"And you think Mathias Sinclair will give us permission to search his land?"

"What I think," Edna pointed out. "Is that no one will dare question a mother visiting her daughter. Nor, a brother his sister. If anyone finds us on Bar S and, we will just claim to be on our way for a visit."

"I don't know about this…"

"Please Sebastian," Edna begged, "Please, help me restore our family's good name. After everything your sister did to tarnish it, I need you son."

"Fine, we'll try it your way first, but if that doesn't work, we are calling a town meeting."

"Anything you say son."

-The devil comes in many disguises-

CHAPTER TWELVE

Trudy woke to the strange sensation of an empty spot beside her in the bed. Alarmed and half wondering if she'd dreamt the previous night, she sat straight up and glanced about the room.

"Mornin' Sunshine," her husband drawled from the wheeled chair to the left of her and Trudy's jaw dropped.

There Mathias sat, buck naked in the cane backed chair that he'd refused for months to use.

"This rope pull thing actually works pretty well. Took me a few tries to get the hang of it, but I managed to get in this chair without falling on my ass," he stated proudly.

Trudy couldn't help herself, she burst into noisy sobs.

"Hey now!" Mathias cried out, holding his palms outstretched. "I didn't mean to wake you. Go on back to sleep."

"I'm not crying because I'm tired you fool, I'm crying because I'm happy," she informed him as she wailed like an infant into the palms of her hands.

"Come on Sugar, don't cry."

Rolling the stiff wheeled chair over to the bed, Mathias stared down at his wife as if she'd lost all good sense. "If that's what you do when you're happy, I hate to see you when you're pleased as punch."

"I'm about to show you pleased, Husband," she announced with a wink, her eyes still misty. "You'd better hang onto that chair of yours."

"I'd rather hang onto you," he whispered just before Trudy stole his ability to think straight.

Heedless of her nudity, Trudy sprung up onto her knees and threw her arms about his neck and nuzzled his shoulder. She loved the spicy scent of his skin and the way he growled when she bit down gently.

As he pulled her into his lap, together they discovered that the chair had more use than originally thought. As Trudy clawed his shoulders and moaned in ecstasy, Mathias knew he was a fool not to have tried it out sooner.

***

Daisy Howard Pylright stepped off the stage onto the dusty boardwalk and curled her lip in distaste. The place hadn't changed much in all the time that she'd been gone at all. How unfortunate.

As the driver unloaded her trunk, Daisy looked about for someone to carry it to her mother's house for her.

"Hm…" she muttered. There were not many men ambling about to choose from. As luck would have it, a tall gentleman stepped out of the building to the right of her. He looked brawny enough to do her bidding.

As he neared to where Daisy stood, she flashed him her most brilliant of smiles and batted her lashes hoping to gain his admiration.

"Ma'am," he greeted with a tip of his hat, but tried to walk on completely ignoring her. Daisy was in shock! No one had ever ignored her before. She was beautiful damn it. Even in her horrendous widow's weeds, she was stunning. She would not have it!

Feigning tripping over an unstable plank, Daisy managed to get the man's attention as she fell to the ground with a false cry.

"You alright there?" he asked Daisy as he helped her to her feet. Looking up into his face, Daisy nearly recoiled at the scarring that marred his cheek. Forcing a smile she nodded and thanked him kindly for his assistance.

"Well then, good day."

"My ankle feels turned," she complained when he once again started to walk off. Gad! What kind of man was he anyway to ignore her?

"Would you allow me to escort you to where you're going?" he asked with a loud sigh and Daisy wanted to brain him with her reticule.

"If you'd be so kind."

"This trunk yours?" he asked and Daisy was glad that the man at least hadn't complained when she informed him that yes, it was.

"Which way are we headed?" he asked as he hefted her heavy trunk as if it were light as a feather.

"Do you know where the Howards live?" Daisy asked. For the truth be known she hadn't a clue at all. Last time she saw her mother, she'd been packing up ready to flee their tiny farm and all that stinking dirt that'd clung to her skirts.

"Any relation to Miss Etta?" he asked his gaze sharply focused on her all of a sudden.

"She's my sister."

"Well don't that beat all!" he crowed with a smile and Daisy's eyes widened. What a peculiar man she thought with a grimace.

"I'm Tex Brody," the man greeted her as if she cared a fig as to who he was.

"Pleasure to meet you," she purred out of habit.

"If you'll follow me, I bring right on over there."

As Daisy followed the man she tried not to pout. Too bad the fellow wasn't handsome it had been too long since she'd taken a lover and until she convinced Mathias Sinclair that she was now ready to be his bride, she could surely use a little diversion.

***

"Here you be Ma'am," Tex announced as he placed the trunk on the ground and tipped his hat. He didn't dare knock, for fear Mrs. Howard would try to run him off again. Better he not soil their family reunion.

The woman whom hadn't stopped rambling off about her own beauty the entire way through town was silent for once as she looked about the place. Tex could tell she was not happy with her accommodations and he had to smother a grin. This woman must be some kind of changeling dropped into the midst of her family bosom, for she could be no sister to his sweet Etta. The women were worlds apart. One day he planned to make Etta his wife and he'd be right glad if the woman preening next to him settled for only writing on the rarest occasion. She was trouble and he could do without any more of that.

Turning away from the Howard dwelling, Tex made his way back to his shop. He was in a hurry to finish the piece that he'd been carving. He planned to give it to Etta the day that he made her his bride.

As whatever –his- name- was walked off, Daisy thought maybe she should do the same. How in the world could she bear to reside in this hovel? Unfortunately she had no funds to go elsewhere, so gathering her nerve, Daisy knocked on the wide door.

"Daisy Lynn! Oh my darling you are home!" Edna cried out as the door swung open and she spied her daughter on the front stoop of her house. "I was just telling Etta not but a few weeks ago that I knew you would be returning to us! A mother knows in her heart when her children have need of her."

"Oh Mama!" Daisy wailed as she was enveloped into her mother's embrace. "Percy is dead. I could not bring myself to write this news to you."

"Dead!" Mrs. Howard gasped. "How can this be?"

"He died heroically, Mama. He died protecting me from bandits," Daisy informed her sniffling.

"Oh my darling, don't go worrying yourself over it." Grabbing a linen square from her sleeve, Mrs. Howard blotted Daisy's eyes. "When you are ready to speak of it, we will. My poor sweetheart!"

"I wanted to come home months ago, but the money ran out. You didn't send me enough, Mama." Daisy sniffled into the square and raised a brow in Etta's direction. "Is that my dress Etta?"

"Yes," Etta mumbled her eyes downcast. She plucked at the folds of the muslin gown uncomfortably. "This was in the rag bin Daisy. I've been wearing it for years."

"I'd rather you asked me before you wear my clothing, even ones meant for rags," Daisy informed her sister, and Etta's cheeks flushed.

"I'm sorry," Etta murmured softly.

"Oh! How wonderful it is to have my beautiful daughter home!" their mother declared happily, ignoring her elder daughter's bullying. "It grows so tiresome having to ramble about the place with only Etta for companionship."

"I love you Mama," Daisy said with a happy smile forming upon her pretty face.

"My precious," Mrs. Howard cooed. "I love you most of all."

Without a thought to Etta, both Daisy and their mother turned on heel and walked arm in arm into the parlor. They began to chatter as if they were long lost friends as Etta stood in the entry awkwardly.

"Oh Etta," her mother looked up and smiled at her daughter.

"Yes Mama?" Etta took a step into the room, happy that her mother finally realized she had not included her other daughter in their impromptu family reunion.

"Why don't you go make us some tea dear? Maybe you can put together something to nibble on as well? Your sister has come a long way; surely it would be rude of you not to offer her something?"

"Oh I am truly famished!" Daisy declared with a pleased grin. "It is so wonderful to be home."

-Great battles often start with small skirmishes-

CHAPTER THIRTEEN

Mathias eyed the apparatus with determination. If he could get himself over to the tub and manage to lower himself into the water, then Mathias would forever grateful. If he failed and fell in, he'd probably end up drowning himself. The risk was great, but if it was one less thing he had to rely on someone for, then Mathias was willing to attempt it.

It had taken Trudy and Annie five trips apiece to fill the hip tub with the steaming water and he was sure appreciative of it. While having his wife sponge bathe him had never failed to entertain him, Mathias longed to the soaking of a lifetime. The muscles of his arms and back felt sore as they were only now being used on a regular basis as he worked about on the rope pulley.

Wheeling himself over to the hip tub, Mathias pulled his night shirt over his head and tossed it carelessly over his shoulder. Starting tomorrow, he was going to be sporting trousers on these legs of his. It would be a struggle to manage, but it was necessary if he were going to push himself out on the wide porch and watch as Trudy hung laundry out to dry. He could hardly wait. After the story that Annie had told him about the last time Trudy tried her hand at wash day, he was looking forward to it.

Grasping the wooden handle to the rope pulley, Mathias unhooked the counterweight and grinned as the rope pulled taut and his bottom rose a few inches in the chair. Yanking on the cord once again, he tried releasing a second bag of sand, this time it did the trick. His muscles strained as he tried to swing himself over the rim of the tub. It was tricky, but he managed to make it into the tub.

Steam still rose from his bath water as Mathias leaned against the rim of the tub and sighed happily.

"You can stop hiding behind the screen Tru, I see your feet," Mathias called out.

"I wasn't peeking!" Trudy cried out as she walked around the wooden screen that Alec had helped Patrick build for him. A thick bundle of toweling in her grip, she approached him apprehensively.

"I brought you some soap," she informed him.

Mathias smirked. The woman had seen and touched about every part of his body at one time or another, yet she still blushed at the sight of his bare chest.

"Look your fill woman," Mathias encouraged with a wink. "I plan on doing the same to you tonight in exchange. I've thought of a new position we can try using that chair of ours."

"Mathias!" Trudy squeaked and threw the soap at him.

"What?" he asked, as innocent as a lamb. "A man has to have something to dream about."

Running the sliver of soap over his chest and arms, he sang a naughty tune about a lady who'd spotted a man so fair that she'd fallen upon him and had her wicked way with him. For effect he changed the lady's name to Trudy and added an extra verse about what she'd done last night upon him with her mouth.

Her eyes wide, she gaped at him in disbelief. This was not the same man that she'd followed back to his ranch. Gone was his defeatist attitude. In his place was a man who was singing dirty ditties!

"Don't act so shy Sugar," Mathias ordered with a chuckle.

"No one has ever accused me of being shy before," Trudy said coyly as she approached the tub and took the soap from his hand.

"Well then," Mathias prompted as he pulled at the ties of her chemise, releasing her breasts for his viewing pleasure. "Why don't you join me in here and we can see how much water we can spill?"

"I thought you'd never ask."

Climbing into the water she straddled his hips and grinned.

"How's that song go again?" she asked archly.

"Let me show you."

Trudy scored her nails down Mathias' back and froze.

The lump on his spine had grown larger, by at least an inch in diameter.

Later she would tell her husband that the reason she'd called a halt to their lovemaking was due to the size of the tub, but that was a lie. The real reason was that she couldn't lie to herself or him any longer. It was time to tell Mathias that it was she that botched his surgery.

***

"Gertie!"

At the sound of that dreaded nickname, Trudy groaned inwardly. Only one woman called her that horrible moniker.

Turning around to face the small, thin woman hurrying toward her, Trudy pasted a demure smile on her face. "Good day Frances," Trudy greeted.

Frances Pritchard was dressed to the eye teeth in finery. Her bonnet was of the best quality, and perched on her beautifully coiffed light brown curls.

"How fortunate that I should run into you this morning!" Frances crowed as she ignored the presence of Annie who remained by Trudy's side silently watching.

"Did you hear that Daisy Lynn Howard is back in town?" Frances asked with a smirk. The action made Frances's small features appear almost rat-like in Trudy's opinion.

"Is she?" Trudy shrugged as if unconcerned. "How nice for her mother."

"She looks more beautiful than before she left town," Frances confided. "Why, I declare that her frocks are the most fetching that I've ever seen in my lifetime.... even better than the ones that you used to wear."

Trudy wouldn't let the likes of Frances Pritchard upset her. The woman just wanted fodder to gossip about, but Trudy would give her none.

"You could not imagine this, but her husband has died," Frances confided to Trudy in a whispered tone. "I wonder how long it will be before she sheds her mourning."

"If you will excuse me Frances, but Annie and I need to finish our errands," Trudy made a move to walk on, but Frances caught her arm.

"Trudy," Frances purred. "I hope you understand why we haven't been around for a visit. I cannot step foot in a home where a fallen woman resides. My reputation you know."

"I understand completely," Trudy replied. "It was actually a blessing that you haven't been out to the ranch."

"Oh? Are things that dreadful there?" Frances asked in a voice akin to hopeful, "Is Mathias causing you trouble?"

"Only the best kind of trouble, Frances," Trudy replied with a smirk. She was tired of people trying to garner whether or not Mathias could perform his husbandly duties. He could and he did it quite well, but she was not about to tell one of her oldest acquaintances that tidbit. People thought she was stupid and couldn't see through their ploys, but she was on to their games. Ever since certain people in town had found out that she'd married Mathias, the first thing anyone asked her about was whether he was 'well.' Let the woman wonder until eternity it would give her narrow mind something to chew on.

"Oh," Frances breathed as she finally caught on to Trudy's implication.

"But, your lack of a visit has saved me from having you thrown off of my property. Good day Frances," Trudy announced as she pulled her arm from the other woman's grasp and continued to stroll down the boardwalk.

"Well I never!" Trudy heard Frances gasp, but she did not bother to turn around.

Trudy was here to accomplish something, and looking backward at her old life, would only hinder her.

"She should, maybe it would loosen the stick in her spine," Trudy mumbled and Annie starting to giggle beside her.

"I have a feeling that by the time we head out of town today, everyone is going to have heard about what you just told her."

"Frances Pritchard is just a nosy busybody like her mother- in- law Florrie. I don't pay the least bit attention to her."

"I wish that I were as brave as you Trudy," Annie confessed in a whisper.

The trouble was Trudy wasn't as brave as Annie saw her. She was shaking in her boots at the thought of coming to town on her errand today. But she was going to do it. Once she asked Dr. Fisher to accompany her back to the ranch to examine Mathias' back there would be no more lies. She'd have to explain to both Dr. Fisher and her husband just what she'd done. Heaven help her, but she was terrified that Mathias was going to hate her and revert back into his old ways.

"When you're finished with your errands, I will meet you by the livery. Baxter has a few new foals that he's fostering, and

I'd like a chance to see them before we head out."

"It shouldn't take long," Trudy agreed as they parted ways.

She just hoped that the man was willing to help. After the way Mathias had acted before, Trudy was sure it might take some powerful persuasion to get him to agree.

CHAPTER FOURTEEN

"I'm confused." Dr. Fisher announced as Trudy poured him a second cup of tea. Thankfully the hotel dining room offered such a thing as a tea service. She'd needed something to keep her hands busy else she'd wring the skin from them in her anxiety.

"You're saying that a lump has formed and continues to grow?" Emery Fisher asked the girl as he added another lump of sugar to his weak tea.

"Yes."

"Is the skin intact? Does it weep?"

"The skin is intact though it feels warm to the touch, there is no pus present."

Trudy Sinclair answered the question without hesitation and Emery found that he liked that about her. He could never abide a fragile woman that would feign the vapors over words such as pus, or blood loss.

In his profession, Emery had come across many women of all backgrounds, but the women of this town seemed to gain his esteem. Well, most of them at any rate. They were strong and independent women that a man would be proud to have at his side. Trudy Sinclair was such a woman, even if she were a tad too self-doubting.

"Will you tell him?" Emery asked.

"I'll have to. It's only right."

When the girl had first come to him with her tale, he hadn't seen the problem with hiding her secret. After all, what was done was done. But then again, Emery wasn't the one who had to live with the secret. Women were fussy about such things as honesty, and talking about every little thing on their mind. Thankfully, Emery had found a woman that valued calm and quiet. Bethany was everything to Emery, so he could somewhat understand Trudy's dilemma.

"I'll come by to see Mathias on one condition," Emery announced.

"Anything!"

"If he requires further surgery, I expect you to assist."

"I can't do that," Trudy denied his request. "I can't bear the thought of hurting him any more than I already have."

Trudy bit her lip and Emery watched her warily and prayed that she wasn't the type of woman who gave into dramatics.

"My father was right; a woman like me had no place doctoring anyone."

"I'm only going to say this once so listen well," Emery lowered his voice and leaned in close. "I happen to be the greatest surgeon known to man," he bragged. "*And*, if I say you're going to assist me, you're going to assist me. As for your father, he was a fool," Emery declared bluntly. "One day females will dominate the field of the physicians. Up north they are already starting to. And you, Mrs. Sinclair, can do anything that you set your mind to. Any woman can, except that contemptible Florrie Pritchard. That woman is as dumb as dirt."

As the woman across from him started to grow weepy, Emery decided it was best to change the subject. He was a gruff man that preferred silence to conversation, but his intended said that he needed to make a better effort to become more approachable.

"Now then," Emery cleared his throat. "What do you think of the practices of leeching? Are you for or against?"

As the woman began to speak regarding one of Emery's favorite debates without pouting over such a topic over tea, he was pleased. It was nice to finally converse with a like-minded individual. It was hard to find a woman that wasn't squeamish when it came to those slimy bloodsuckers. Yes, he thought with a nod, he liked this woman and was determined to fix her man before she reverted into a watering pot and became useless to him. He had a hard time garnering friendships, and wanted to keep whatever associates he could manage to find.

***

With time to waste before she had to meet up with Annie, Trudy decided it high time to pay a call on her new sister in law. She told herself that she was only going to visit the dresses that she could no longer purchase, but she knew the truth.

Trudy just couldn't bear to think of Mathias estranged from his sister the way she was from Sebastian. It was high time she did something for the man she loved, even if it meant being pleasant to the fiery headed troll that sewed the finest dresses in the territory. Well, everybody had to have one redeeming quality, and sewing was Serena's.

The bell above the door tinkled as she waltzed into the shop and a wave of nostalgia washed over her as she eyed all the pretty fabrics.

"How can I help y—" Serena Sinclair came out of the stockroom and froze as she spied Trudy.

Trudy in turn tried her best not to gape at Serena's belly. It was quite large for such a tiny woman. Trudy's hand shot to her own stomach as she thought about what a blessing it would be to carry Mathias' child. Maybe one day there would be the possibility.

"How are you?" Trudy greeted after long minutes of the two just staring at the other.

"I am well. How is Mathias?" Serena asked.

Trudy could see the sheen of tears in the other woman's eyes. She knew just how she felt. There was a bond between siblings that even anger and misplaced notions couldn't sever.

"Stubborn as ever," Trudy answered with a shrug. "He's finally using the ambulatory chair that your mother ordered." He was getting quite good at it too, Trudy thought with a satisfied grin.

"That's wonderful!" Serena exclaimed with a sudden smile.

"You should come and see him for yourself," Trudy invited.

"I don't think that he'll want me there," Serena declined sadly.

Trudy bit her lip. If she was already going to be inviting Dr. Fisher to the ranch without Mathias' say so, she might as well go all out. "*I'm* inviting you to a Sunday super Serena. Alec too, though you can tell him there won't be any molasses biscuits."

"Oh no!" Serena chuckled. "You found Alec's weak spot. His love for molasses is quite legendary in our family."

"I could tell."

As Serena waddled closer she held her hand out, before Trudy could ask just what in the world the woman was doing, the bell once again jingled announcing they were no longer alone.

"I want a new dress!" a voice complained.

"You're in mourning Daisy," Etta Howard voice could be heard scolding whomever she was with. "You aren't supposed to wear light colors."

As the light clicking of heeled boots sounded, Trudy froze in horror. She was coming face to face with the woman that Mathias had loved for so many years.

With no other option than darting into the stockroom like a frightened rabbit, Trudy stood her ground. She watched as a raven haired beauty sauntered up with a practiced pout. Trudy knew that look; she herself had been born practicing that very expression.

"Good day, Mrs. Wentworth, Mrs. Sinclair. This is my sister Daisy," Etta greeted, as she introduced the woman by her side.

"So, you're the little dove that Mathias was so fortunate to marry." Daisy's tinkling laughter grated on Trudy's nerves, but she warned herself to remain calm. She was no longer the foolish young woman that she once was.

"Etta, even *you* are dressed better than this!" Tossing a black curl over her shoulder, Daisy made a pouty face. "Mathias must surely be in dun territory, if he can't afford to properly clothe his young bride."

"Mathias is doing just fine, Daisy Lynn Howard! I will thank you to keep your opinions on my brother's state of affairs to yourself," Serena Wentworth snapped irritably. One hand passed over her swollen belly; she shifted uncomfortably and tapped a swollen foot.

"Little Serena?" Daisy gasped. "Not so little anymore are you dear?"

"*Daisy*!" Etta hissed.

"You look like a right cow!" Daisy burst into laughter and pointed a finger at Serena's girth. "I thank our good Lord that I never got with child. Goodness, I would hate to be that huge. Are you cumbersome dear Serena? You sure look it."

"Daisy!" Etta chided her sister. "Serena is with child. You should not say such things."

"Oh do shut up Etta. Go back to cowering in the corner little mouse! No one wants to hear from you." Daisy turned her disdain onto her sister. "I can say what I want."

"You are a vicious crow, my brother is lucky that he avoided shackling himself to you." Serena's nose rose in the air as she stated her opinion.

"Yes, I see that he's done so well for himself…" Daisy smirked.

"We were blessed with his choice in bride, and I will not have you disparage Trudy any longer. Get out of my store now!"

Trudy stared in shock at the fiery red head that she called sister-in-law. Serena had defended her and even pretended to be happy with Mathias marrying her… could she have a fever? Trudy nearly reached out a hand to feel the woman's forehead, but her attention was diverted as Daisy shoved her sister Etta roughly in the back.

"Come on Etta; let's get out of this pitiful shop. I have too many well-made dresses to bother with these *rags*."

"You go. I have business to discuss with Mrs. Wentworth," Etta refused.

"Fine," Daisy snarled. "Stay behind, but don't you for one moment think that I will not inform Mama of your spite, Etta."

"Do what you must," Etta replied before turning her back on her hateful sister.

"Very well done Etta!" Trudy exclaimed as Daisy fled the store as if her bustle were on fire.

"It was about time Etta!" Serena seconded and took Etta by the arm. "Come, let us sit and you can tell us what it is you need."

"Should I leave?" Trudy asked unsure.

"No, please stay," Etta managed though it was clear that she was embarrassed by whatever in the world she needed to discuss. "I could truly use the advice of two married ladies."

"Then please," Serena prompted. "Tell us how it is that we can help you."

"I need your help…" Etta broke off with a gulp before trying once again. "I need help in catching myself a husband."

***

Daisy Lynn Howard stood in contemplation. Her brightly colored parasol tapped against one palm as she accessed the situation. She needed a strategy and quickly. Time was running out for her. She needed money, and she needed it fast. Her mother had let her down. She had confessed only last night to Daisy that she had no money. What sort of foolish woman ran out of money? Daisy's own lack of funds was not her fault. It was Percy's plain and simple. If only her thoughtless husband had not gambled everything away. Why Daisy would still be in high society, and far away from this peasant filled town. If Percy were not such a lousy cardsharp, Daisy would never have had to return to this hovel.

Across the street a group of cow pokes stood leaning against a railing watching her. Daisy knew they liked what they saw, so she puffed up her bosom a bit more and smiled their way. She was bored, and it felt good to toy with the dupes. Her dull sister was still shopping inside that pathetic excuse of a dress shop that Mathias' family owned, and Daisy was tired of waiting on her.

Imagine the likes of that Serena Sinclair speaking to her that way! How uncivilized these bumpkins were.

Etta had changed quite a bit in the last few years, and Daisy was not impressed one little bit. Why, just this morning her sister had refused to dress Daisy's hair for her. This new backbone that her sister was growing needed to be crushed before too long. Daisy would not put up with Etta's defiance for much longer. In fact, it was time that Etta knew just where she stood in life. Her plain countenance would only hinder her in life. Etta would eventually wind up alone and needing to live off of Daisy's largess, it was better that she learned now what Daisy would expect from her in the future.

Daisy watched with a pout as Etta finally left the confines of the shop. Her sister was smiling brightly as she strolled up the boardwalk. Stopping two stores up, Etta peered into the window of the candle makers. Daisy yawned. Etta was truly the most boring of souls. Imagine a woman ogling candles the way one would boots and bonnets!

Daisy was about to make her presence known to her sister, when that tall brute of a man came out of the store and bowed over her sister's hand.

"Hmmm," Daisy murmured as she watched her sister beam up at the man who'd carried her trunk. This was not like Etta at all. Daisy's eyes narrowed as she watched the man tuck Etta's hand in the crook of his arm and escort her into the shop.

"Well, well…well," Daisy said clucking her tongue. She just might have found the way to snap Etta right back into her little ole place after all.

-Fear can cripple the bravest of men-

CHAPTER FIFTEEN

She was a coward.

Trudy had promised herself that she was going to tell him the truth tonight. Instead, she found herself in the throes of passion, and who could think straight enough in that state to tell the truth?

It wasn't all her fault though, as the man had an agenda of his own. As soon as she'd climbed into the bed, he'd whispered all sorts of naughtiness in her ear, making her squirm with need.

"Mathias," she moaned as she leaned back and rotated her hips. The move was one that brought them both pleasure.

"Yes, love, just like that," he encouraged, gripping her hips with greedy fingers.

As Trudy found her pace and began to rock harder against his swollen cock, Mathias suckled one budded nipple into his mouth and bit down, sending her over the edge. She came apart in his arms, crying out his name.

As he found his own release, Mathias could've sworn that she murmured 'I love you' under her breath. It was probably just his imagination, but the thought made his heart quicken in his chest.

Trudy had been acting strangely all evening and he'd no clue as to why. Something had to have happened when she went into town with Annie this morning.

Wrapping his arms about her, Mathias kissed the top of her head and asked, "What's going on in that mind of yours, Tru?"

"I don't know what you mean," she denied but it didn't fool him. He could tell that she was hiding something from him. He could feel it in his gut.

"Tru—"

"Fine," she huffed. Her head shot up and she gave him the look. The very one that said he wasn't going to rush her into revealing something that she wasn't ready to.

"Go on," Mathias prompted.

"I saw Daisy Howard today," she announced glumly, and Mathias had to bite back a grin.

"Daisy? When did she get back into town?" he asked with a straight face. It was not easy as her eyes narrowed at him at the sound of the woman's name falling from his lips.

She was jealous. Mathias nearly sighed with relief. He'd thought maybe she was keeping something else from him…something much worse.

"I wouldn't know when she got here, but she's here."

Judging by her tone, Trudy was not thrilled that Daisy had landed back in Liberty. As for Mathias, he couldn't care less as to what Daisy did. He wanted naught to do with her. Trudy had nothing to be worried about on his part, but it touched his heart to know that she was jealous. Did Trudy actually think the woman would fight her for him? The idea was laughable but sweet.

"Is that all?" he asked.

"No," she sighed. "I asked Dr. Fisher to come tomorrow to look at your back."

When Mathias stiffened she rushed out to explain. "I think you may have an infection on your spine. There is a lump that keeps growing and I'm worried."

"What did the doctor say?"

"Just that he's going to come and take a look."

Mathias yawned and pulled Trudy closer. He wasn't going to worry about it until the doctor told him that he needed to. Nothing good ever came from worrying.

***

With the dawn, Trudy found herself face first into the porcelain basin that she'd used for Mathias' sponge baths. Heaving up everything in her stomach, she felt weak and unsteady on her feet as she collapsed back on the bed.

"Tru?" Mathias stirred.

"Go back to sleep," she ordered with a groan.

"What's the matter?" he asked sleepily.

"My belly aches," Trudy confessed.

She was so worried about what Dr. Fisher would find when he examined Mathias that she'd made herself sick.

"Come here," he held his arms out and she immediately went into his embrace, seeking his comfort.

In a few hours Dr. Fisher would be there, and Trudy would have no reason not to confess her secret to the man that she loved. She just hoped that Mathias would be forgiving enough to hold her in his arms after she told all.

-Miracles exist if you look hard enough
to see them-

CHAPTER SIXTEEN

The doctor waltzed into the room a
short time after Mathias had finished with his
morning meal. Trudy, following at his heels,
carried a stack of clean linens and wore a look
of unease about her.

Tossing his bag onto the foot of the
bed, the man approached Mathias without so
much as a greeting.

"Take off your shirt," he demanded.

"Holy! Doc, I didn't even think you
liked me," Mathias joked.

Dr. Fisher shot him a glare, and shook
his head in disgust.

"I see you're in a better mood from the
last time I examined you."

Opening his bag Dr. Fisher dug around. Pulling forth an instrument that looked like a shallow cup attached to twin tubes, the man placed the ends into his ears and smirked. "Let's see if your good humor can last through today."

With the help of his wife, Mathias found himself naked, lying on his stomach as the doctor placed the cup shape apparatus onto his back.

"So, what do you call that thing you're wearing anyway?"

"It's a device to listen to your lungs. Now, if you'd kindly shut your trap, I can get to it," Emery informed him with a sigh. "Doctoring would be so much easier without the patients," he announced to the woman pacing by the bed.

Her movements were distracting him so Emery ordered her to hand him the toweling and find a corner to go sit in until he needed her.

Long minutes passed as he listened to the lungs, finding them free of rasp, Emery nodded in satisfaction. There was always a risk of fluids building in the lungs with a body that was bed bound. If it had been the case, there would be no attempt at surgery today, as it would probably kill the patient. But as his lungs seemed clear, he could get to work.

Exchanging his earpiece for a small dark bottle and a square of gauze, Emery straightened with a smile.

"And now, for my favorite part of surgery," he announced as he dumped a healthy portion of the liquid onto the cotton.

"What's that?" Mathias inquired.

"Helping you to stay quiet so that I can work," Emery informed him.

Placing the square over Mathias' nose and mouth, he encouraged him to breathe in. It only took a few moments before Mathias was completely out.

"And now," Emery declared happily, "we get to work."

***

"Doctor?"

Emery Fisher held up a hand to the nervous young woman at his side, indicating that he desired silence. He studied the line of his patient's back. The incision that he would have to make wouldn't have to be a long one, but it would be far longer than the well healed scar that already marred the skin.

"Hold the lantern a bit higher will you?" Emery requested.

Trudy lifted the lantern as Emery picked up his scalpel.

It was infection, no doubt about it. With the first incision into the bulge the nauseating smell of rot escaped and Emery fought the urge to gag. He loved this part of his work! Judging by the damage to the underside of the epidermis, Mathias was lucky he was alive. Nothing short of a miracle had kept the infection from spreading to his brain and killing him. They were lucky that they found this now.

Removing as much infection as he could, Emery doused the wound with water and soda mixture, then once again with clear water just to be sure.

"Now that the infection is sorted out, let's have look to see what is going on in his spine shall we?" Emery more or less was talking to himself, he did that often, but the woman at his side responded with a nod.

"Surprisingly, nothing was severed in his spinal cord," he pondered allowed. "I see a swollen contusion about the spinal artery but nothing that shouldn't heal given time."

"There was that piece of bullet that I wasn't able to remove," Trudy reminded him as if he'd possessed a faulty memory. Emery sighed, he'd let that go. He told himself she was just worried for her man at the moment and hadn't meant to doubt him.

"Yes, I will remove it as soon as I see what else is going on in here."

It seemed to take hours, but in actuality was less than one before Emery located the last of the tiny bullet fragments that had been left inside, and with Trudy's help, stitched him up.

"All in all, a splendid surgery," Emery announced as he washed the blood off his hands in the shallow basin of water that she'd provided. "I would say he's better off now that the fragment is no longer pressing upon his nerves."

"What of the infection?" Trudy asked. "Will it return?"

"Assist me in rolling him over," he ordered her.

"I don't think the infection will return. In fact, I suspect he will feel right as rain soon enough."

"He will walk again?" Trudy asked hope filling her voice.

"Only time will tell my dear," Emery said patting her hand gently. "The human body is a phenomenal thing. But, I believe that he may have a good chance to fully recover."

"Thank you sir," Trudy spoke around the tears clogging her throat.

"Follow my instructions carefully for the next few weeks and I will come and check back on him," Emery ordered as he grabbed up his tools.

"Yes sir," she nodded.

"And Trudy?"

"Yes sir?"

"When I come next, I have a new specimen of maggot that I want to show you. You know the pigmy's use them as not only a food source but to seal wounds. Quite interesting don't you think?"

***

Mathias woke with a pounding head and a heaving gut. A basin was shoved under his nose just in time. The force of his retching made his head feel like it would pop off.

"Mathias," Trudy crooned as she rubbed his shoulder gently. "It's just the after effects from the Chloroform. It will pass in a moment."

Lying back against the pillows, he was grateful as she helped him sip a small amount of water. Mathias felt as if his mouth were filled with dirt.

"What did the doctor say?" he managed to ask.

"Dr. Fisher got out all of the infection, and he even thinks you may walk again!" she cried out happily. He would have too, had his head not begun to swim so violently and his stomach lurch once again. This time she wasn't as quick with the basin.

Their celebration would have to wait until his stomach settled and she could change her dress.

-True joy is counting your blessings-

CHAPTER SEVENTEEN

Two Sundays later; Trudy threw her first dinner party as Mathias' wife.

With the help of Annie and her husband, the night had gone rather well. As the three couples sat around the table laughing, Trudy sent a sidelong glance in her husband's direction. He was enjoying himself immensely, and she was glad.

She'd been battling tears since the moment he'd pulled his sister into his embrace and allowed the expectant woman to cry all over him. What in the world was wrong with her lately? She was turning into such a watering pot.

Never in her life had she thought she'd be pleased to share a meal with Serena, but there she was, offering the other woman a slice of pie prepared by Trudy's own fingers.

Too soon for her liking, the night was coming to a close.

Annie, hand in hand with Patrick, headed off to their home as Alec and Mathias wandered to the porch to enjoy a cigar, leaving Trudy and Serena alone in the dining room.

"Trudy," Serena spoke breaking the uncomfortable silence. "You have done wonders for Mathias, and I thank you."

Tears pricked at her grey eyes and she faced Trudy. "Tonight was the first time that I've seen him smile, let alone laugh, in a long time. You have been good for him."

"Mathias enjoys laughing at my expense, but I thank you for the kind words. They are so unlike you, are you feeling well?"

"Me? You are the one that hated me first, Trudy," the other woman declared with a laugh.

"I never actually hated you Serena," Trudy confessed as she picked up the empty plate in front of her guest.

"Yes you did," Serena argued with a chuckle. "And, I wasn't quite fond of you myself."

"Yet here we are, related by marriage," Trudy remarked with a grin as she finished stacking the plates.

"Yes, here we are." Serena made a move to rise in order to help, but Trudy waved her away.

"Sit, a woman in your condition needs to be off of her feet as much as possible."

"I feel so large and uncomfortable. I know that Alec must think me horrendous, as fat as I am."

"You are with child, you're supposed to grow large and horrendous," Trudy quipped with a sly smile. "Besides, I was always jealous of you, and seeing you like this makes me feel quite content."

"Vicious cat," Serena hissed and they both began to chuckle.

"Trudy!" Serena suddenly gasped and held her stomach.

"What is it? Is it the baby?" Trudy went instantly to Serena's side and knelt by her chair.

"I don't know! It's a sharp pain in my stomach, and my back aches," Serena admitted with a wince. "It's been aching all day long."

"I believe you may be in labor," Trudy informed the woman who had begun to grip the table and moan.

"You have to help me. It is too early, I still have nearly a month until the baby is due," Serena sobbed in fear. "We have to make it stop!"

"Shhh," Trudy soothed. "The baby is just in a bit of a hurry. Babies come early sometimes. Everything will be fine."

"Are you Su—" the last of the statement was cut off as Serena, unprepared for the next contraction, released a shriek loud enough to rattle the windows.

"Serena!" Alec Wentworth came barreling into the room. "I heard your scream."

"She's starting her labor," Trudy informed him.

"We need to get her back to town!"

"Alec," Serena moaned in pain.

"Help me lift her," Trudy ordered the man. "Let's get her to the wagon."

Together they assisted Serena to her feet, and got a few steps from the entryway, when a gush of liquid puddled about the laboring woman's feet.

"Holy s—" Alec bit off a curse. "*What is that*?"

"It's the baby's water Alec. It's completely natural, though I fear that there is no time to get her to town now. She will have to deliver here," Trudy informed the father to be over the sharp wail his wife had just let out. "Let's bring her up upstairs and make her as comfortable as we can."

"Do you know what you are doing?" Alec asked nervously as he lifted his wife into his arms.

"She'll have to help deliver our baby," Serena managed to speak around the pain. "There's no one else."

"Serena, I—"

"It's okay Trudy, I trust you," Serena said as she reached out and squeezed the reluctant woman's hand. "We can do this."

With a brief nod to her husband, Serena was carried into Trudy's room and laid gently upon the bed. As Trudy unlaced the boots that encased her swollen feet, Alec stripped the gown from his wife.

"Urgggggh," Serena groaned and began to complain about the nonstop pain radiating in her lower back.

"Rub her back," Trudy ordered as she went toward the open doorway.

"Where are you going?" Alec cried out as she made a move through the entryway. "You can't leave her!"

"I need some supplies to help with the birth," Trudy answered without looking back, so great was her hurry.

She was halfway down the wide staircase, before she realized that Serena Wentworth was actually trusting the most precious thing in her life in her hands. That fact scared the curls right out of Trudy's hair.

***

"You have to push Serena!' Trudy ordered as she winced in pain. Serena had grasped two large handfuls of her hair, and was pulling it roughly.

"God love a goose!" Serena squealed as another pain hit her, and she released the hold she had on Trudy's hair.

"Hold my hand Sugarplum, squeeze tight," Alec soothed his wife.

Serena barred down and screamed loud enough to wake the dead. The poor dear tried her best, but the baby was not appearing. Trudy checked her progress and stilled. She felt a tiny foot. This was the worst outcome she could have expected. The baby had turned in the womb, and was now in the breeched position. The delivery had just escalated in danger, and Trudy felt panic rise in her gut. She pushed it away, for panicking would neither do Serena, nor her, any good.

"Are you okay now Serena? Has the contraction passed?" Trudy asked rising from her haunches.

"Yes,' Serena panted. Her body was covered in perspiration, and her face looked nearly purple with bruises from straining.

"Alec, please come with me," Trudy asked of the man who was holding his beloved's hand and grunting alongside of her, as if he, himself, were in labor.

"What's wrong? Where are you going?" Serena called out worriedly.

"Serena just rest. We will be back in a second." Trudy assured her.

"What is it? What is wrong?" Alec pounced on Trudy as soon as the door shut behind them.

"Alec, the babe has turned inside of her," she explained gently.

"That is it?" Alec sighed in relief. "I am sure that the boy was probably a little cramped in there. Does this mean she will be in labor even longer?"

"Men." Trudy shook her head and pinched the bridge of her nose.

"It means she is in trouble doesn't it?" Mathias spoke from the darkened hallway, and Trudy jumped a foot in surprise.

"What are you doing here, Mathias?" Trudy turned on her husband with hands on her hips. "You should be in bed, you just had Doc Fisher digging around in your spine not but two weeks ago!" She fussed at him.

"I'm just so happy to be walking, that I can't stay in that bed any longer than I have to." Mathias smiled a crooked smile at her and Trudy's heart leapt. He really needed to stop doing that! She needed him to go back to being his surly, stubborn self, so that she could concentrate.

"Pardon me! My wife…did you forget about her?" Alec snapped. "Tell me what the hell is going on!"

"Serena is in trouble Alec, the baby can become stuck. He can suffocate inside if he is not born soon, and Serena can bleed to death," Trudy said bluntly, and wished she hadn't, when he turned sheet white and doubled over as if he were punched in the gut.

"She will be fine. I know my sister." Mathias walked stiffly forward with the help of his cane, and patted Alec on the back in comfort. "Come on, you know how stubborn that girl is."

All at once, Alec rose and shrugged off his friend's hand. "I will go get Doctor Fisher; he's probably at the Rotgut Saloon."

"There is no time to get Doc Fisher, and before you suggest it, Sebastian gave up his practice to run the bank!" Trudy cried out. He did not understand what she was trying to explain to him.

"We have to do something!" The mayor snapped as he paced wildly. "I can't lose her! I can't lose my wife."

"I will help her, but you need to calm yourself Alec. We need to keep our wits about us right now."

"My son is killing her! How can I keep calm?" Alec roared.

"You need to find a way," Trudy said sternly. "Now let's get back in there. Mathias you go get yourself into our bed."

"Should I let Annie know what is going on?" Mathias asked, stalling. He was obviously reluctant to leave with his sister in danger.

"She won't be much help right now," Trudy said waving away the suggestion. "Let her sleep. We can send for her if we need to."

Dragging the mayor into the room with her, Trudy never bothered to see if her husband had followed her instructions and went back to their bed. There was no time, for Serena was screaming in agony and in desperate need of assistance.

"Serena," Trudy informed the laboring woman calmly. "I need to try to turn your baby."

"Ooooomph," Serena grunted in response before clutching her heaving belly and releasing another piercing wail.

Trudy washed her hands in the basin once again before going to sit between Serena's splayed legs. In hushed tones, she explained everything that she was doing to the frightened woman and terrified father-to-be.

"This is going to hurt," Trudy informed her sister in law.

"Just do what you have to do," Serena ordered in between gasps.

Trudy prayed that she was doing the right thing. There was too much blood for an average birth, and she had only witnessed her brother deliver one breech baby in all the time that she had attended him.

She needed a miracle right this moment.

Wincing as Serena's body began to contract again; Trudy pushed her hands deeper into the birth canal and tried to grasp the baby. She nearly burst into frustrated tears when she realized that there would be no way that she could turn the child. The babe would have to be born breach.

"Truuuudy!"

"I know Serena, I know this hurts. Just give me a second; I have to try to bring the baby's other foot down," Trudy explained.

"You're doing good Sugarplum," Alec encouraged as he supported his wife's back. Kissing her temple, Alec praised her efforts and told Serena that he loved her. There were tears glistening in his eyes as well, and Trudy smiled briefly as he cleared his throat and ordered his baby to quit scaring the daylights out of his parents.

"Here we go," Trudy declared as she felt another contraction building in Serena's belly. Moving quickly, Trudy searched for the little one's hidden limb. The second tiny foot was a bit higher, nearly to the child's waist, so Trudy gently brought that foot down so that Serena could now push the babe out. She worried briefly about the cord wrapping itself about the babe's neck, but had no time to do anything about the thought, as the babe began to slide free from its mother's body.

"Push Serena!" Trudy yelled excitedly.

With a mighty scream and a good deal of yelling from Alec Wentworth, a tiny, squalling babe was brought forth into the world.

"It's a girl!" Trudy announced happily as she began to clean the child and cut the cord that connected the tiny child to her mother. Wrapping the baby girl in swaddling, Trudy handed her over to her father. She still had some work to do in order to make Serena more comfortable.

"A girl! We have a girl Sugarplum!" Alec Wentworth crowed happily as Trudy placed the child in his arms.

"Trudy!" Serena began to wail in pain again.

"Stop!" Trudy cried out, but Serena could no sooner stop pushing than she could stop herself from breathing.

Trudy hurried over and expected to assist Serena in expelling the afterbirth, but was shocked by what she discovered.

"Sweet lord!" she gasped.

Another baby was ready to be born into the world. This time, the child was coming head first, to Trudy's relief. The crown of the second baby's head was already showing.

The laboring woman started to pant and instinctively push and her husband's head shot up.

"What's wrong Serena? What's wrong with her?" Alec demanded of Trudy when his wife could only groan in pain.

"She is having another contraction."

"But, I thought those would stop when the baby came out?" Alec asked as he rose from where he was perched next to Serena on the bed. Hurrying forward, the baby still clutched in his arms, Alec made a nuisance of himself.

"They will once the second baby is delivered," Trudy said with a shrug. Her attention centered completely on the task at hand.

"Twins!" Alec bragged to his wife, whose face at that moment was nearly violet from the strain. "Maybe it's a boy?" he called out to Serena who took that moment to scowl up at him. She obviously did not care the sex of her children, just that they stopped causing her pain.

The second baby slipped from its mother's womb with less drama than the child before, but not as much as the baby that followed suit. In the end, Serena had worked hard to birth three red faced babies. The three were quite small, with very little hair and healthy lungs. Trudy had wished that she had ten arms after the birth of the girls. With Alec's help she had managed. Together they had washed the babies and changed Serena's bedding and gown.

Three babies! Trudy had never seen the like. She had heard about the phenomena occurring once to a family in New York, but she had never witnessed such a thing in her life. The Wentworth's would be the talk of the territory for some time to come.

"All girls," Alec gasped. His arms filled with two of his daughters, the third little darling was cradled within her mother's loving embrace. Alec looked as if he were in shock.

"Are you disappointed?" Serena asked Alec, and Trudy could not help but eavesdrop on his response. She knew that her own father would have been livid with his wife for daring to fail to produce a male.

"Not in the least," Alec pronounced as he leaned in and kissed Serena's mouth tenderly. "I now have three beautiful girls to remind me of why I love their mama."

Trudy busied herself with gathering up the soiled linens. Tears pricked the backs of her eyes. The sweet, honest answer that the mayor had given his wife, made Trudy feel a little sad inside that her own father had not felt that way.

Planning to get a warm glass of milk for the new mother and giving the new parents privacy with their infants Trudy walked to the doorway.

"Trudy!" Serena called out.

Turning, Trudy faced the tired woman.

"Thank you," Serena said with a wide smile.

"No need to thank me, we're family."

-Serpents slither amongst the rotted vine-

CHAPTER EIGHTEEN

Three days following the birth of his tiny nieces, the Wentworth's finally managed to head off to their own home in town. While he'd miss watching Tru coo over the squalling bundles, it was nice to have a bit of quiet once again about the place.

Managing to wobble awkwardly into the main room, he sank gratefully into his wheeled chair. He didn't use it often, but when he became overly tired, it was nice to have the thing around. It also came in handy when he sat at his desk figuring payroll.

He wondered where his wife had gotten off to this morning. She'd been up and about for hours, and he'd no clue what she was up to.

The light patter of footsteps sounded and Mathias smiled.

"So, there you are, Sugar," he murmured as a hand snaked about his neck from behind.

"Here I am."

Throwing off the arm as if it were a serpent, Mathias swiveled the chair about and faced the intruder.

"Why are you here, Daisy?" Mathias asked. His tone suggested that he could not care less whether or not she answered the question.

"Can't an old lover stop by for a visit?" she asked with a pout.

"No."

"Mathias, I want you back!" Daisy leaned over and gifted him with the view of her pushed up breasts. Mathias figured her corset must be laced pretty darn tight to achieve that look. It was a wonder the woman could breathe at all.

"Daisy," Mathias muttered in disgust. "Why don't you go take your games elsewhere?"

Smiling coyly, she ran one nail down his cheek. Daisy was not going to take no for an answer. "Don't you remember how good it was between us? Think about how good we were… we can be like that again."

"You know I am a married man now Daisy, you had your chance."

Mathias leaned away from her. The smell of her perfume was turning his stomach as she rubbed against him in the invalid chair. "You chose to leave me and marry your fancy man."

"He's dead now Mathias! Nothing is keeping us apart anymore. Nothing can stop our happiness."

"As I said before, I am married now Daisy. Even if I wasn't, nothing on God's green earth would make me take you back."

"I know all about your little bride. I know that it's not too late to annul your marriage. I know that you haven't touched her in a husbandly way." Daisy's hand strayed down his chest and toward his lap.

"Stop it!" Mathias snarled grasping her before she could make contact with his lower regions.

"It's because you can't be a real man to her isn't it? Your infirmity won't let you rise to the occasion will it?"

"Shut your mouth," Mathias growled.

Daisy smirked as she tore her arm from his grip. "I can help you with that Mathias. I learned quite a bit being married to Percy. I can give you the pleasure of an experienced woman in your bed," she promised. "I still think about those nights I snuck out to be with you. Don't you remember our first time together?"

"Daisy," Mathias huffed. "Just leave."

"Do you think of me, Mathias? Don't you wish that I hadn't left?" Sinking to her knees before him, Daisy laid her head on his lap and sobbed. "We could be happy once again!"

"You did leave Daisy," he answered with a sigh. "That's all that matters. You left and I've moved on."

"Please," Daisy begged. "Let me make it up to you."

Rising up she threw her arms about his neck and pressed her lips to his before he could fight her off. Gripping her arms he prepared to push her away.

As fate would have it that was the exact moment his wife chose to walk into the room.

***

"Tru!" she heard him call after her as she ran from the room.

Stumbling through her tears, she made it to the door all the while vicious laughter rang in her ears.

Seeing Mathias holding the woman that he loved in his arms had shattered her soul. Her heart felt as if it was ripped in two and she knew that soon it would be time to leave him behind. She would find a way to leave without making herself appear anymore pathetic.

"Trudy!" she could hear him call from the distance, so she ran faster. Heading toward the thicket of wooded land to the west of the Bar S, she broke through the clearing intending to cross onto the O'Malley's land and seek refuge with them. It would burn her pride to beg for their aid, but she couldn't go back home.

Stumbling, she fell to her knees weeping and held her stomach. Once again, she had another secret to carry. But no matter what, she would never regret her child. She'd only come to the realization that she was increasing last night when she'd mentally counted back her courses and realized she'd skipped two.

Long minutes passed as she sat there on her knees and thought about what she'd just witnessed.

"Trudy?"

Her head shot up in confusion.

"Sebastian? Mama?" she shook her head in disbelief.

"What are you doing here?" she asked as Sebastian helped her gain her footing.

"Better question is, why are you crying," Edna asked her lips pursed.

Before she could answer the question her husband came tearing through the bush as fast as he could manage with the assistance of his cane.

"Trudy!" he panted, "It's not what you think. She threw herself into my arms."

"Oh yes, and you had to fight her off!" Trudy snapped furiously. Pointing one accusing finger in his direction she sobbed, "I could tell how hard you *fought* against her lips!"

"What have you done to my sister?" Sebastian asked angrily.

"What are *you* doing on my land?" Mathias shot back.

"Answer the question damn you!" Sebastian shouted as he pulled a gun from the waistband of his trousers and pointed it at

Mathias. His hands shook uncontrollably as he tried in vain to steady his weapon.

"What did you do to my sister?"

"Sebastian?" Trudy gasped. "Where did you get that gun, and why do you have it?"

"It's for our protection," Sebastian answered with a shrug. "We need it while we search for the bags."

"What bags?" Trudy inquired. Was the entire world going mad?

"The bags of money that fool Joe Vernon stole from the bank. It's rightfully ours and we mean to find it," Edna informed her daughter. "We've been searching for weeks now."

"Put the gun away Sebastian," Mathias stated evenly.

"Shoot him!" Mrs. Bixby screamed furiously at her son. "Kill him Sebastian," she ordered once again, as Sebastian remained frozen.

"Mama," Sebastian turned to look at the furious woman standing near him. His hands shook as he tried to keep the gun steady. "I don't think this is the way to avenge father's death."

"He took and ruined your sister! Look at her face, she's been crying! Are you going to let him tear apart the rest of our family

Sebastian?" Her face was turning florid as she demanded once again. "Kill him, and Trudy can come back to us. We can be happy again Sebastian, just the three of us. We'll find your father's money and start over."

"He didn't ruin me, Mama!" Trudy cried out angrily at the suggestion. She would have charged at her brother, but Mathias pulled her roughly behind his body in order to protect her.

"Happy? Do you honestly think that killing me will make either of your children happy? Mrs. Bixby, I think you are overcome with your grief," Mathias took a slight step backward and came up against the edge of the tree line, Trudy's body preventing him from further retreat, he pressed into his wife.

His cane hit the ground, and Mathias paid no attention to it. "Your daughter is my wife, everything I own is hers. You are more than welcome to it, but have your son put that gun down."

"Mama, please listen," Trudy begged as she tried to peek over his shoulder. "You can't keep poisoning Sebastian like this. Papa is the one that stole from the Sinclair's not the other way around. He had planned to bankrupt the Bar S so that he could foreclose on Mathias." Trudy directed her comments to her brother now. "Haven't you found the discrepancies yet in Papa's ledgers Sebastian? He was stealing from the whole town just to prove he was better than the rest of them. He has been funneling funds to the Hill boys."

"*The Hill boys*?" Sebastian repeated in horror.

"Yes," Trudy confirmed with a nod. "They are trying to gather another army together, and our father was aiding them. I knew he was supporting those fools, but I didn't know he was stealing from the town to do it."

"No one would have ever known about that if you wouldn't have been disloyal to your papa," Mrs. Bixby spat. "We gave you the best of everything. The best clothes, the best foods, and this is how you choose to repay your family? You are siding with this… this… dirt groveler? You betray us."

"You gave me the best of everything except love and morals, Mama. You, who sits on church leagues and charities, the one who walks through those sanctuary doors every Sunday and pretends to pray for the less fortunate," Trudy said as she tried to side step Mathias, but her husband was having none of that, and once again blocked her movement.

"You are a hypocrite Mother, and as much as I love you, I never want to be like you."

"You weren't complaining as you spent the money that your father stole."

"You knew? All this time you knew what Papa was doing?" Trudy asked stunned. "Do you realize what the Hill boys are capable of? They are murderous serpents."

"I knew. But as long as I was quiet, Thomas stayed by my side." Turning to face her daughter, she smirked. "And talk about lies. Does he know the truth?"

"What truth?" Mathias asked as she focused his attention at the shaking gun directed at his middle.

"Go ahead and tell him daughter dear," Edna prompted. "Tell him that it was you that ruined his spine."

"Mama!" Sebastian shouted. "I'm sorry Trudy; I hadn't meant to tell her."

"What's she talking about?" Mathias questioned his wife.

"It was me, not Sebastian, that pulled the bullet from your spine," she explained reluctantly. "I'd been helping Sebastian for some time because of the tremors in his hands," she explained with a wave toward her brother whose hands were indeed showing his affliction. "I wanted to do something to help you after the way you saved my life, but more than that, I wanted the chance to prove myself, to be better than what I was."

"Trudy!" Sebastian called out, "it wasn't your fault, it was unavoidable."

With a shake of her head Trudy continued, "I misjudged the damage and the bullet splintered as I tried to remove it from your back. The piece that I broke off was too hard to remove. It was too close to an artery to even try."

"Tru, baby, that doesn't matter to me," Mathias assured her as she sobbed.

"I was afraid to tell you, I thought that you'd hate me!"

"I could never hate you," he assured her. "I'd hold you in my arms right now, except for this gun trained on me."

"Please put the gun down Sebastian!" Trudy begged her brother. "I love him and I can't bear to lose him."

"Then, as far as I am concerned, you can die alongside your husband," Mrs. Bixby said genuine tears formed in her eyes. "You leave us no choice, Gertrude. We have to avenge your father's death."

"I won't hurt Trudy," Sebastian refused the demand.

"That's right, you won't," a smug voice stated calmly.

The cock of a pistol from behind Sebastian had the young man stiffening, his eyes as round as moons, his mouth dropped open. His mother, spying the danger behind her son squawked furiously.

"Put the gun down now," Patrick Culver demanded as he ignored the irate woman. "Don't make me end you boy. My wife doesn't like when I have to kill people."

"Do as he says Sebastian," Mathias urged the young man gently. "I know that you don't want this to go any further than it has to. This isn't like you Sebastian."

"We have nothing left," Sebastian gasped out as he dropped the gun onto the dirt pile and held his empty palms outward. "There is no way to save the bank. We have lost everything. I am so sorry, but my mother convinced me that it was your family's fault that we were ruined."

"It is their fault! If the Sinclair's wouldn't have thought they were better than your Papa, he would have been allowed on the council. He would have been happy, instead of always trying to find ways to fit in," Mrs. Bixby sobbed, clutching her abdomen. "Do you know how much I suffered because they would not accept him? Neither one of you ungrateful children know how many beatings that I took because I failed to win over the perfect Charlotte Sinclair!"

"That is not Mathias' fault," Trudy whispered as she escaped from behind her stunned husband and knelt by her mother's side on the ground. "Mama, you were being controlled by Papa, just as Sebastian and I was. Papa is gone now and it is time to move on. He can't hurt us any longer."

Wrapping her arms around the broken woman, she pulled her mother tightly and rocked with her. Trudy's chest ached as her mother wept violently.

"What are we going to do, Sebastian and me? We have no money; the house will be gone as soon as the town knows we cannot repay the money that was stolen from the robbery, let alone once the truth about what your father was doing comes out."

"What should we do with pair of them?" Culver asked. "Should I call in the sheriff? Take them to town?"

"Mathias—" Trudy began to fret.

"I think we can work this out amongst ourselves, don't you think so?" Mathias asked. Turning to his mother in law, he cocked a brow. "After all, we're all family here."

"You would just let us go?" Sebastian uttered in shock. "After all the things we've done to you?"

"What I'm doing, I do for Tru," Mathias began. "I'll give you the money to go wherever you want to. It will be enough to survive on for a while, at least, until things die down around here."

"Mathias, no! You need that money for the ranch," Trudy argued.

"Tru, let me handle this," Mathias countered. "Family takes care of family."

***

"There were so many things that I overlooked. There were so many lies that our family had to maintain to protect Papa."

"So tell me the truth about your father," Mathias rubbed Trudy's hand reassuringly as they walked back toward the house.

"Papa had a bad temper," she began in a whisper. "There were many times that he would allow his fists to show me the error of my ways."

"Didn't your mother ever help you?"

"No," Trudy answered shaking her head. "Mother never interfered with Papa. She chose to ignore his tirades. If his anger spilled over to her, she would punish me as well."

Mathias smoothed the hair from her eyes and tucked her head under his chin. He did not rush her, but let the story unfold in her own time.

"There were times that I had to lie to my friends and tell them that I fell to cover the truth of a bruise. Times that I had to push people away so that no one could ever guess that Papa was not as loving as he pretended to be. Papa told me even as a young girl, that I was worthless to him. But he swore that the day would come, when I would marry well and would be able to earn his approval."

"You were his daughter, that alone should have earned you respect," Mathias said sharply.

"I was twelve when my father first started bringing men to the house. He never let them touch me, but there was something about the way they looked at me that I knew something was different in their visits." Trudy laughed; it was a hollow sound that raised the hairs on the back of Mathias' neck. "He groomed me at a young age to know my value. He told me that if I did not please him, he would gift me as a bride to someone with enough gold to line his pockets."

"That is disgusting," Mathias spat out, unable to keep quiet.

"It is the way of the world, Mathias. Women have been forced into marriages since the Lord himself walked the earth beneath our feet. I was just lucky that my papa had been too greedy to settle," she said patting his chest.

"No daughter of mine would be treated that way," Mathias said emphatically.

"I was actually somewhat happy with my spinsterhood until papa forced me to take part in the bridal bid. He wanted me to land Alec Wentworth so badly," Trudy said with a bitter laugh. "I was always such a failure to him, and I wanted to make him proud of me… just once. Some things never change."

"Trudy, you devalue yourself by saying that. You've got more gumption than most men, and more heart than you think you have," Mathias informed her kissing the top of her head gently. "A cold woman would have let me die that day. You never once mocked me, nor allowed me to wallow in self-pity."

"I could never do that!" Trudy gasped.

"Why? Why couldn't you do those things Trudy?" Mathias prodded.

"Because…because, I love you!" Trudy cried out.

"I know sweetheart. But you couldn't do those things because you are good inside. Even if you do not see it in yourself, I see it in you."

"You see what I have been trained to show others Mathias," Trudy denied. "I am not real. I do not even know who or what I am on the inside… not anymore. I don't deserve you Mathias. I never did," Trudy said as the tears that she tried to hold back escaped, and traveled down her face. "Just let me go."

"Why? Why do you need to leave?"

"Because, it's my fault. The pain my father and I caused your family can't be undone," Trudy said sniffling as they walked into the barn. She hadn't wanted to go into the house where that woman waited, so the barn seemed the only logical place to hold their conversation. "You can walk again. You don't need me anymore."

"Who says that I don't?"

"Mathias—"

"Trudy," Mathias chided gently as he drew her to him. "You're not responsible for your father's actions."

"What about my own?" Trudy asked. "I helped him cheat, I helped him steal. I stood by and lied for him and I schemed alongside of him just to gain his approval," she confessed. "I conspired against your own family."

"And you have changed. Everyone else has forgiven you, now it's time you forgave yourself sweetheart."

"I can't."

"I love you Gertrude May Sinclair," Mathias declared as he cradled her face in his wide palms. "Look at me woman."

"Mathias," Trudy began. Her voice shook and she gulped back tears. "Don't say it if you don't mean it."

"Do you honestly think that I would lie to you about this?"

"Not lie. But, maybe try to make it easier for me to stay with you." Trudy shook her head in denial. "If I go, you can have everything Mathias. Daisy wants you back, she told you so herself. You could have what you always dreamt of, without me."

"I don't want Daisy," Mathias stated bluntly.

"You built this house for her, she meant a lot to you, she—"

"This house was not built for her. It was built because of my foolish pride, damned it all!" Mathias snapped cutting her off.

He was irritated that Daisy had sunk her claws into his wife and that Trudy had allowed Daisy to poison her mind with her venom.

"It was the idea that I wasn't good enough for the faithless jade that spurned me on, that much is true, but it wasn't out of love," Mathias denied. "I love you Tru, just you."

"How can you love me after everything that my family did to you? You couldn't walk for the last five months because of me!" Trudy cried as she tried desperately to free herself from his grip. She wanted to run away and hide from the shame she felt inside.

"Tru," Mathias sighed. "Don't you know that I would die for you willingly? That I would willingly throw myself in front of that bullet for you all over again? Don't you realize I was half in love with you even before the robbery?" he asked, as he drew her even closer into his embrace. "Do you think that I just happened to run into you on the streets of Liberty so many times out of coincidence? I yearned for you, well before I woke up naked and defenseless in your arms."

"Truly?" Trudy gasped as she paused in her efforts to free herself from his embrace.

"I know that I made you feel unwanted, and I tried to scare you off, but the truth was that without you, I would never have recovered." Mathias paused to kiss her tenderly before he continued on. "Without you Trudy, I would have withered in that bed and died, unable to see that life still had meaning. But, it only has meaning with you behind me."

"Mat—"

"You Trudy, are my strength, you are my spine. You, Trudy Sinclair, are the only real love that I've ever felt."

Brushing the tears from her cheeks tenderly, Mathias refused to allow her to shut him out. "You were the bride that I was meant to have, though I did not always see it. You are the one that I have always wanted."

"Don't leave Trudy," he begged. "You have a life here, a home here, and people that love you. Don't walk away because of what your brother and your mother mistakenly did. There is forgiveness enough in this town for all three of you, and when your family returns, they will find it. Of that I have no doubt."

"I will stay on one condition," Trudy promised, smiling through misty eyes.

"Anything sweetheart," he promised.

"I want to name our baby George if it's a boy." Trudy requested.

"Our baby?" Mathias grinned in response to her demand.

"That's what I said." She folded her arms across her chest and narrowed her eyes in her husband's direction, when he just continued to grin instead of responding to her news. "Well? What do you say about that?"

"I say let's celebrate!" Mathias declared with a whoop, and pulled her gently down to the ground.

The thick pile of straw broke their fall, as he rolled atop of her. The soft snuffling of horses in their stalls mingled with the sound of the now pouring rain as Mathias did his best to love every inch of his beautiful wife.

*-Community and faith are the strongest
of foundations-*

CHAPTER NINETEEN

June

The shouting began at sundown. The beating of pots and whistles followed suit. Wagons pulling up to the ranch were filled with trays of sweets and heavy bags of staples. Sugar, flour, and linens were amongst the gifts, along with whiskey, lots and lots of whiskey from the council.

"What in the world?" Trudy muttered as she made her way to the window and watched as the hordes of townsfolk unloaded their goodies.

"It's an old fashioned shiveree," Mathias announced from behind her as he watched with a smile on his handsome face.

"A shiveree?" Trudy gasped, "For us?"

"It's their way of welcoming you Tru," her husband whispered against the side of her neck as he stooped to kiss the spot that never failed to run shivers up her spine.

"Welcome me?" Trudy laughed. "After everything my father did to them? They have so little now, and they are giving it to us?"

"Liberty has always been a strong community, together we'll get past this and with the help of each other we will all rebuild. The sale of your parents' house will go a long way to helping those families that your father stole from."

"I think it is wonderful that Alec has decided to buy it and donate it to the town. I wonder what they will use it as."

"All I know is that he made darn sure the council wasn't going to get a say in it."

"We should probably get down there and welcome our guests," Trudy remarked as yet another wagon pulled in through the gates.

"We will… in a moment, but first, kiss me Tru," Mathias whispered in her ear. "Kiss me as if you're mine forever."

"Well lucky for you sir, I am."

***

In the darkness, under the aged oak tree that had a new set of initials carved in its trunk, a couple of adversaries stood apart from the festivities.

"Well I suppose you're going to demand that kiss I owe you," Winnie grumbled as she watched Mathias Sinclair claim his own bride's lips passionately. She knew she'd lost the bet with the man standing beside her and could no longer put off the inevitable.

"Well, Miz Winnie, you seem to forgotten your debt is two kisses this time," Fergus informed her solemnly. "I'd hate to think that you'd be considered a welcher."

"I'm no welcher, you old goat!" she snorted.

"I know that, but I'd hate for you to fall the way of the untrustworthy. I'm just doing the gentlemanly thing by making you pay up."

"Gentlemanly? Ha!" Winnie huffed, "A gentleman wouldn't have asked this price to begin with."

"Oh!" Winnie muttered when the man beside her remained undaunted, "Fergus, if you want your kiss here it is."

As Winnie puckered her mouth and leaned in, Fergus turned his head so that her lips met the skin of his leathered cheek.

"What in the heavens? I thought you wanted your kiss?" she sputtered.

"You see, I've given it some thought, and I think you're right. A gentleman should only kiss his lady after they've said some vows, so I'm thinking that a kiss on the cheek will have to do for now."

"Vows?" Winnie repeated wide eyed as the old man did his best to drop to a knee before her. His gout only letting him get as far as a hunker before he fell over, but it was still quite romantic as Winnie helped him back to his feet.

"Winnifred Lawrence, will you do me the honor of marrying up with me?" Fergus asked her

"Are you daft?" Winnie asked shocked. "At our ages? We're a little long in the tooth for that don't you think?"

"Win, I may not be able to promise you a long life together, but I can promise you the time we're together will last an eternity. Five minutes, five years, five lifetimes, any time that we get together should be cherished and made the most of."

"People would laugh at us," Winnie complained.

"Sweetheart," Fergus chuckled, "marry me, and show them all that people our age can still make magic. Let me be your last love on this earth, for you Win, sure are mine."

"Oh Fergus!" Winnie cried. "Yes, yes I will."

Tears flowed down her soft cheeks as the smiling Fergus fished in his pocket for a handkerchief to offer.

"You know Fergus, I still owe you one more kiss," Winnie reminded her suitor.

"Ah lass, I'll content myself to waitin' like the gentleman I am."

"It's a good thing I'm not a gentleman," Winnie announced before taking matters into her own hands. And there in the moonlight, with the town that they both loved celebrating behind, the pair shared a kiss that would make the youngest of lovers envious. Lusty lady that she was, Winnie wasn't going to let the man think she was going to let him off easy... he was going to be spending that time he kept talking about, showing her just exactly what kind of magic they could make together.

Love knows no age, nor time. For the heart never really grows old when it's in love, it only beats stronger when it finally meets its match. Winnie and Fergus were proof of that.

Epilogue

Trudy could swear that half the town had shown up on her door step that afternoon, and were now gathered in her parlor. At least the female half were settled in quite nicely and devouring Annie's honey biscuits. The male lot, were currently holed up in the barn hiding out from their womenfolk. They were no doubt drinking large quantities of whiskey from the new still that the council boys had talked her brother- in -law Alec, into building for them. While the women had contented themselves with tea, Trudy could surely use a spot of whiskey at the moment.

Trudy laughed as Serena's triplets crawled about the floor. Seven months old now they were just starting to get around on their own. And boy could they move fast! Little Willow was scooting about like a worm across the floor heading for the door.

Serena was such a good mother, that Trudy hoped that she could learn from her friend. Trudy had some doubts about her own ability due to her own mother's lack of maternal affection. Every now and then, Trudy thought about the woman who'd birthed her and few good memories would surface. They'd gone to visit with her Aunt Estella in New Orleans and turned the visit into a permanent move so that Sebastian could be cared for by a doctor in the area.

She missed her brother and the closeness that they had shared. Sometimes, she even missed her mother, but she understood that they needed to stay away for a while.

"How are you feeling Trudy?" Annie asked from her seat beside Trudy.

"Like an overfed sow," she answered with a pout causing laughter to burst out amongst the women.

All of the women present were here for one reason, to impart their maternal wisdom and lend support to the heavily pregnant woman, who was only hours away from giving birth. Trudy expelled a deep breath and tried to get comfortable on the divan. Her back hurt and she felt swollen and miserable. Soon it would be time for her to retire to her bed and prepare for birth, but not yet. She did not want to disrupt the bonding that was going on all around her.

"Can you imagine three babies at once? Lord, I hope history doesn't repeat itself with you Trudy," Annie Culver spoke as she pried a hair pin from one baby's hand and handed it over to a grinning Serena Wentworth.

Trudy was grateful that Annie was now coming out of her shell and allowing others to see what a funny, remarkable woman she really was.

"You are one strong willed lady, Serena," Annie said with a laugh.

"Well, I have a lot of help. Between Alec, Mrs. Wyatt, and Alec's mother Bethany, the babies are well looked after." Serena waved away the praise and lifted her tiny daughter into her arms. Placing the baby in the hastily built area that had been constructed to barricade the babies in Trudy's sitting room, she gathered up her two other darling girls, and placed them on the blanket next to their sister who had finally stopped crying.

Georgina, also known as Georgie by her papa, looked at her sister Penelope with mischief in her eyes, before proceeding to make a grab for her sister's rag doll. The three Wentworth girls after starting a tiny baby brawl, all started howling at once making Trudy wince. As adorable as the three red headed babies were, Trudy had no desire to hear her nieces wailing.

"You make everything look so easy. I have one baby and I can barely keep up with her," Melody O'Malley teased as she spooned a portion of stewed apples into her own nearly year old daughter's mouth. "Though soon, Gabriel and I will be giving you a run for your money on daughters."

"Do you mean?" Serena gasped, and everyone including Trudy, who was fisting the folds of her gown in pain, turned to stare at the tiny blonde.

"Yes, I'm expecting again," Melody O'Malley confided with a smile.

A chorus of squeals of happiness and one lone squeal of pain sounded, as congratulations were said.

The population of Liberty, Texas was growing rapidly with each passing month. Doc Fisher, who over the last year had been knee deep in deliveries, complained good-naturedly about having to stick around in town, due to what he called the baby bloom. He was not fooling anyone; Emery had finally found a home in Liberty and he couldn't be happier. After only four months of courting Bethany Wentworth, Emery Fisher had eloped with the woman. Today, he was to be assisted by his new wife. They had yet to arrive, and Trudy was becoming nervous. She hoped her birthing experience did not turn out as traumatic as her sister-in-law's had been.

"Everything all right in here Tru?" Mathias stuck his head in nervously and asked.

"I think it's time to go upstairs now," Trudy informed her husband in a near pant.

Her face was red, and she looked awful, though Mathias would never make the mistake of repeating his thought aloud. Not with so many women giving him the eye.

"I will help you," Mathias offered, limping into the room and ignoring the cooing sound his sister was making in his direction. Tru was his wife damned it, and he wanted to help her through this birth situation that she faced. She had stayed by his side for all those hellish months that he'd been trapped in that bed, it was his turn to care for her.

Ignoring her protests, Mathias lifted Trudy into his arms and proceeded to carry her to their room. Placing Tru on the wide bed, Mathias helped her from her clothing and into her night dress. As she reclined against a mountain of pillows, moaning and thrashing her head, Mathias began to become nervous.

"I think you might need to deliver this baby, Mathias," Trudy grunted out in between shallow breaths. "I'm scared," she confessed.

"Doc Fisher will be here soon. Just hang on sweetheart," Mathias lifted her hand and placed a kiss on the ridge of her knuckles. He immediately regretted the action when she damn near broke his fingers in response to a particularly strong contraction that had suddenly hit.

"I don't think there is much time," Trudy squealed. "My water just broke!"

"*Oh my God*!" Mathias stared down in horror.

He'd faced outlaws, crooks and thieves the lot of them, but he had never felt so terrified in his whole life. Not even when he'd been held at gun point facing death, had he felt his heart pound so hard that he feared it would explode.

In the end, Doc Fisher and his wife had showed up in plenty of time to help deliver their son. Serena and Charlotte had stayed by Trudy's side, as Mathias had paced nearby the door. Melody had stayed in the front room keeping a watchful eye on the babies that were blessedly now napping.

The womenfolk had tried to shoo him from the room, but Mathias wouldn't allow them to. He wasn't going to let anything happen to his wife, if she needed him, he was going to be close by. Every now and then, he would get closer to where Doc Fisher stood, turn pale, and then wish he hadn't seen what he'd just saw. Once, Bethany had to stop helping her husband to walk over and pinch him in order to keep him from fainting dead away.

How in the world did women do this sort of thing and still remain civil to their menfolk? If he were a woman, he'd probably shoot the first man who looked his way with a twinkle in their eye.

At the first squall of indignation from the newest member of the world, Mathias felt a lump build in his throat. Rushing to where the doctor stood cleaning off the babe, Mathias watched as Doctor Fisher handed the boy over to Bethany to be swaddled, before going back to assist Trudy in delivering the afterbirth.

"A boy!" Mathias happily informed his wife with a pleased nod.

He would have been just as happy to have a daughter, but Trudy had insisted the child would be a boy, and that he would be named after the two men that had meant the most to Mathias, the man who'd given Mathias life and the other man who had saved it.

He was small, but judging by his angry cries, little George Patrick Sinclair had a healthy set of lungs. Tears of joy formed in Mathias' eyes as he stared down at his son. The miracle he never thought he'd be blessed with. He would always miss his father, but holding little George in his arms, Mathias felt as if the old man was still with them.

All of the women now stood gathered around the bed. They each praised Trudy for a job well done, as they helped change the bedding and her into a fresh gown. Trudy felt a ring of love form around her, and she was grateful. For all the years she'd pushed real friendship aside and treated others spitefully to please her father, she thought she'd lost her chance at real acceptance. Instead she found the power of forgiveness and a bond with the women of Liberty, Texas that would never be broken.

"I'm going to take our son out and show him off to the men," Mathias said proudly as he pressed a soft kiss to his wife's brow.

"Don't be gone too long," Trudy begged tiredly. She did not want to part with her family for even a second, but she understood her husband's pride. Though he was puffed up and acting as though he had delivered little Georgie from his own body whilst in the midst of a cattle stampede. Men!

"I never thought that I'd see the day," Serena said with a laugh as she watched her brother exit the room in a rush. "My brother all settled down with a family and not a single sour expression has crossed his face in months."

"Trudy," Charlotte Sinclair said with a press of a kiss upon Trudy's cheek. "You have given me back my son, and now, a beautiful grandson to spoil. I can never thank you enough," the widow spoke softly. Her eyes wet with unshed tears, Charlotte continued, "I wish George were here to see all of our grandbabies."

"I miss George too," Trudy said with a wistful smile. George Sinclair had been the father that she'd always wished she could have. He'd taken his last breath four months prior and the thought of his passing still brought tears to Trudy's eyes.

"You have definitely been blessed Charlotte," Bethany remarked. "To have both of your children wed and happy, a woman could ask for no more. I fear that Hunter is never going to settle down like his brother has. "

"He will dear," Charlotte patted her friend on the arm with a chuckle. "The menfolk around these parts always take a bit longer to settle themselves. But, when they finally do, they make their mamas proud."

"You know, there is no reason why we can't help things along a bit for Hunter," Melody spoke from the corner where she was refolding a stack of cloths that were destined to become nappies for little George.

"What do you mean?" Serena asked as she eyed her industrious friend.

"Well, maybe this town needs another mail order bride around the place? Look at how well it turned out for Gabriel and me?" Melody smiled a blissful smile and Trudy had no doubt that the other woman was thinking about her handsome husband who was waiting on driving Melody home to their neighboring ranch.

"Somehow I doubt Hunter would agree to this plan of yours Melody," Trudy said with a yawn. She was growing weary. Having little George had plum wore her out.

"He doesn't have to know anything about it." Melody explained patiently, "Fergus and the boys could arrange a few brides for Hunter to choose from. After all, the council swore they would never host another bridal bid again, but they never promised to stop matchmaking."

"So, we make him think that it was his idea in the first place," Serena purred.

As the women began to plot against the unknowing sheriff, Trudy felt her body relax. Her eyelids felt heavy, and it was becoming hard to concentrate on the chattering around her.

When Mathias opened the door to his room, he noticed two things straightaway. One, his wife was sleeping soundly while the women around her were in a heated argument. The second thing he noticed was that every woman present looked guilty as sin. When he asked them just what was going on, they all seemed overly interested in studying the tips of their shoes. Not wanting to be bothered with anything other than watching his wife sleep, Mathias nicely, yet firmly, ushered the ladies from the room. Kissing his mother goodbye, he nearly had to pry the baby from her arms.

Once the feminine flock was gone, Mathias placed tiny George into the cradle that he'd spent so many months carving, and climbed into the bed next to Trudy.

He realized that it wasn't his resumed ability to walk, albeit unsteadily, that made him whole as a man. It was the love of the woman lying by his side that really fulfilled him.

Mathias realized that even before the shooting he was just a shell of a man living with a bitter heart. There had been an empty loneliness that he had refused to recognize... until Trudy. Now, he felt like there was something to wake up for in the morning. Trudy made him actually look forward to the future. She made him feel alive. And life... well, life was the most beautiful, precious gift he had ever been given, right next to the gift of Trudy. God must have truly listened to his prayers after all. For the first time in a long time, Mathias was grateful. He was thankful the good lord saw to it that he was saddled with the bride that he had least wanted, because only God knew just how much Mathias had truly needed her.

The End

Note from the author

While Mathias's injury to his spine ended up a temporary one, many people of all walks of life are permanently injured. My story is not to make light of that fact, nor give false hopes to those affected. Everyday life is a struggle for those with spinal cord injuries, and I can only hope to honor the strength and determination that it takes for any disabled person to work around life's obstacles.

While researching about such a sensitive injury I had the privilege of learning firsthand about the subject from some lovely members of a (SCI) support group. I discovered the many different areas in which the spine can be damaged, and how it can affect the body in different ways. The differences ranged from some confined to wheel chairs to others able to take small steps, but each person had a story of their own about how they cope.

Depression tends to set in for those who have not been given the tools and training to cope with their new circumstances. Often times, their care providers and loved ones bear the brunt of the patient's frustration. Males in particular seemed focused on feeling like 'half' the man that they once were. In their lives, hopes and dreams seem to be unattainable to them without proper guidance and counseling to help deal with their disabilities.

Which brings me to the one topic of discussion that seemed to pop up the most, sex. This is what I learned: A spinal cord injury (SCI) affects many areas of life. You may have to make some changes in how you are sexually active, but you can still have a fulfilling sex life and even father/ carry a child. Some people believe that sexual intimacy is the same thing as the act of intercourse, but that is far from the truth. A loving, committed relationship and a strong determination to want to share a soulful connection with another being is the true meaning of intimacy.

I wish that in my story, it is apparent how trust and true intimacy can build a love that can endure anything.

A special thank you to those who explained the true "mechanics" of love to me. My only hope is that more money will be spent on spinal cord repair research, and that one day those affected, will be able to take those precious steps again.

-Becca

A Bargain Bride

By

Rebecca De Medeiros

In a time when the west was wild...and the men were wilder... There came a challenge in the small town of Liberty, Texas. The objective in mind: Marriage. Bets are placed, and a race to the altar begins.

Rough and tough rancher Gabriel O'Malley had never met a challenge he could not handle... until now.

Fed up with his grandson's brooding ways, "Pops" O'Malley takes matters into his own hands, and orders a mail order bride for him. Besides wanting the best for Gabriel, there was a little matter of a bet going around that the old man was determined to win. The only problem was, his stubborn grandson was digging his heels "spurs deep" in and holding onto his bachelorhood ruining all of his grandfather's well laid plans.

Gabriel, furious at his grandfather's conniving ways, was determined to rid himself of his unwanted "bride". He was going to live his life on his own terms come hell or high water, and settling down was not something he planned to do. Even if he did lust after the woman who shows up on his doorstep.

After the death of her parents, Melody Williams was left with nothing but her baby sister to see raised and an eviction notice on her door. She thought that finding the advertisement for a mail order bride was her lucky break. That is, until she meets her groom. Statues are friendlier than this hombre.

But Melody is also stubborn. No one is going to stop her from making a home for her sister, least of all the sexy, grumbling rancher she has come to marry.

Sparks will fly, tempers will flare, kisses will be had and shoes will be thrown...As the battle of the sexes begins. Can love blossom? With the help of a bunch of wily old men, the town of Liberty is counting on it.

But not everyone is hoping for a happily- ever -after for the couple. From the shadows, evil lurks waiting to strike the ranch. Will it all be destroyed before their new life together can even begin?

A Betting Bride

By

Rebecca De Medeiros

Welcome back to Liberty, Texas...

Alec Wentworth town mayor and all around nice guy, has a big problem. A problem called marriage. A group of elderly matchmaking men that run the town council have decided it is time to lasso the bachelor and drag him to the altar. The plan is simple, put the mayor up for auction and let the brides bid on him. The men are pinning their hopes that more of the bachelors in town would follow suit.

Alec is a man with a scarred past, one that he hides behind flirtatious banter and roguish charm. His devilishly handsome looks don't hurt him one bit either. But he isn't going to go willingly to the altar…he is a man with a plan… he just needs his longtime friend Serena, to help him out.

Serena Sinclair has loved Alec secretly for years, but enough was enough. It was time for her to move on with her life and leave her plain-Jane spinsterhood behind in her dust. Alec may need her help in thwarting the hordes of ladies who want to become his bride, but she needs his help in teaching her the art of seduction.

What starts out as a few innocent kisses, and one night turns a friendly game of poker into something a bit more wicked… the pair find themselves forced into a hasty marriage. Just in time for the ghosts in Alec's past to resurface in his life. Will the new couple find contentment? Or will a cruel plot and a scorned admirer ruin the joy they could find together?

Shotgun Groom

By

Rebecca De Medeiros

Olivia Montgomery is on the run for her life. Her stepfather, having control of her fortune, has plans to do away with her before her twenty first birthday so that he can have it all. Olivia, having no plans on being his next victim, flees in the night from her mansion in New York. She heads out west, where they say a man can get lost for years, without ever being missed. She is hoping to hide long enough to avenge her mother's death.

Mac Kincaid, bounty hunter turned rancher, has one last job to complete before he can retire and raise his young ward on the land he owns. When Olivia's stepfather offers Mac a fortune to track the girl down, Mac jumps at the chance to get ahead for once in his life. What he hadn't counted on, was running headlong into a fiery Olivia, and everything he thought he knew about the job, changing before his very eyes.

One shotgun, a stormy night, a crazy scheme and some hasty I do's, make for one heck of an adventure as the reluctant newlywed Mac, and his strong willed bride Olivia, seek refuge on his ranch.

As the pair stumble blindly onto the path of unknown danger, will they find their journey leads to true love? Or will evil triumph before they have a chance to recognize what is right in front of their noses?

Also for sale on Amazon

Contemporary Romance

Toddlers and Tycoons

By

Rebecca De Medeiros

Maggie Fairbanks has life summed up in one word: Difficult. After her sister and her deadbeat brother- in- law clean out Maggie's bank account and take off for parts unknown, she is left holding onto nothing but a diaper bag and a heaping helping of toddler sized trouble.

Between her job as a waitress, and trying to put herself through college, Maggie needs to find the extra cash in order to keep her tiny niece and nephew from going into foster care or worse... going back to live with Maggie's selfish mother and her alcoholic father in their rust bucket of a trailer. With nothing left to her name, Maggie takes a job working as a housekeeper for an eccentric old man and his grandson. But more is going on under the surface on the ranch than just dirty dishes, and it just may wind her up in more trouble than she can handle.

Maggie's decision to take the job on the Calhoun Ranch was going to change her life in more ways than one. If Elias Calhoun, patriarch of the Calhoun family had any say in it, the job would be permanent as in for life... Elias has his eye on Maggie for much more than just as his housekeeper, he wants to see her matched up with his hard headed grandson Lucas, and not even the pesky FBI agents hunkering down on his spread, are going to stop him from achieving his goal.

Lucas Calhoun, grandson to the eccentric oil tycoon has his hands full. With juggling the ranch, his family's oil company, and the terrifying death threats aimed at his hard headed grandfather, Lucas doesn't want more chaos thrown into the mix. And chaos was just what Maggie Fairbanks would bring him, along with two babies in tow. Unfortunately, Lucas can't just send her away; he needs her too much, though he won't admit it...even to himself.

When a situation calls for Lucas to propose a temporary marriage to his spirited housekeeper, he never suspects just how much he would gain from doing so, or what he stands to lose...maybe, his very own heart.

With danger just around the corner, could falling in love with a temporary wife be any crazier?

Printed in Great Britain
by Amazon